Leftovers

Kevin Densmore

Published by Kevin Densmore, 2024.

LEFTOVERS

First edition. December 25, 2024.

ISBN: 979-8230943242

Written by Kevin Densmore.

Also by Kevin Densmore

A Series To Die For
A Carnival To Die For

Scary Things Happen in Lakewood
Scary Things Happen in Lakewood
Scary Things Happen in Lakewood 2
Scary Things Happen in Lakewood 3
Scary Things Happen in Lakewood 4

Stories to Inspire and Tales that Terrify
Stories to Inspire and Tales That Terrify.
Stories to Inspire and Tales that Terrify (Volume Two)
Stories to Inspire and Tales That Terrify.(Volume Three)
Stories to Inspire and Tales that Terrify (Volume four)
Stories to Inspire and Tales that Terrify Vol.5

Standalone
Strange 80's State of Mind

Savage 90's State Of Mind
The Devil's Missing Children
What the Rain Washes Away
Sweet 70's State of Mind
Pesky Little Sleeve Hearts
One Night At The 4/26
Journal Of A Lost Boy
Sick Metal State of Mind
April & Zeus
To The Shadows and Back
Gary
Leftovers

Table of Contents

I would like to dedicate this book to my eighth grade English
Teacher: Mrs. Creighton

Thank you so much for believing in me ma'am

"....Leftovers in their less visible form are called memories. Stored in the refrigerator of the mind and the cupboard of the heart...."

---Thomas Fuller

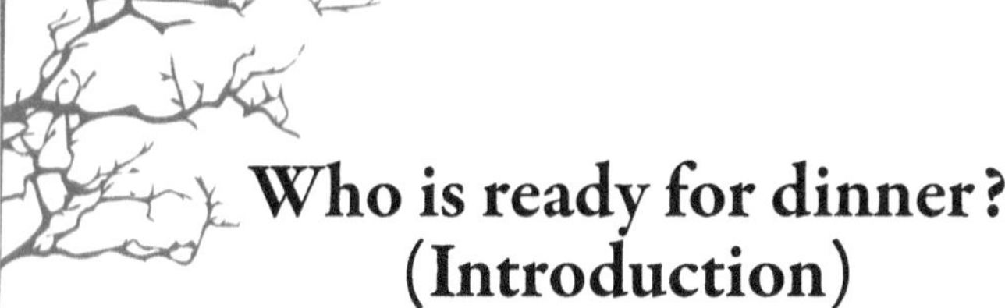

Who is ready for dinner?
(Introduction)

Hi friends, how are you guys doing? I am so glad to see all of your smiling faces today. I am happy that you decided to purchase this book and join me through another collection of stories. But this collection is special.

Why is it special you ask? Well these stories you are about to read were stories that I either cut from previous collections or canceled out right. Some are even old. Like over thirty years old. And now they have their chance to be read. I even decided not to have anyone edit them. Just to keep them pure. After all this is a collection of stories from my past. Why make them look new.

I've done a collection like this once before. In a book called "The Devil's Missing Children." Well after a couple more years I now have enough leftover stories that I can fill another book.

Each one of these stories have been retouched, some rewritten, yet all of them ready to be read. Not all of them can be winners of course. You might find some of them stupid or pretentious which was why I never released them in the first place. Of course there are some real gems here. But I am my harshest critic so hell you may like these stories and just love them.

And yes I snuck in some old forgotten poems this time around, because why not?

Anyways I want to thank all my family and friends who supported me through this project. I want all of you to know that I will never stop writing. And to my small group of fans, I want to thank you for your loyalty. You really make this fun. I do this for you. Well you and of course to clean out the clutter in my head.

As always with my anthologies there will be a fine section in this book that gives a brief story behind each of these stories you are about to read. A little peek behind the curtain if you will.

Well that's it. The table is set. The plates and the food look familiar, but I am sure you will be happy with what is on them. Let the madness begin. And thank you so much for enjoying this feast with me. And as always.

Toodles,

Kevin

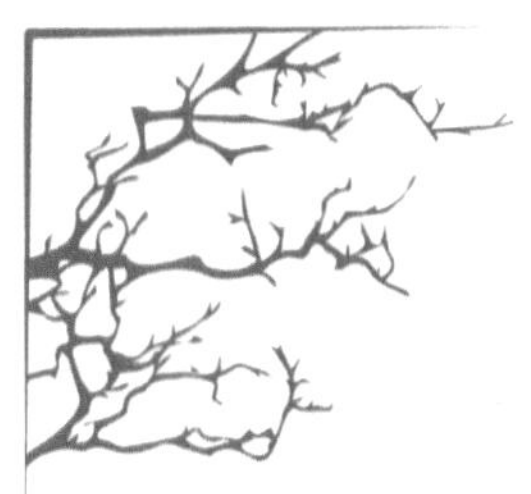

Toy

To call Keith a tad bit obsessive would be to take things lightly. Because when it came to toys, especially those deemed collectable, he was more than just obsessive.

Keith had started his collecting at the young age of twenty five, upon discovering that the toys from his childhood were starting to turn a profit. Which annoyed him. Because the toys he saw at flea markets and other various specialty antique stores were fetching large amounts of cash sometimes totalling in the thousands. Toys he once owned. Toys he just donated.

Knowing he could do nothing about the loss of revenue from the toys he onced owned he decided to start purchasing the toys that were popular now. At first it was just a couple of random purchases here and there. It soon snowballed into one or two purchases every paycheck. Before long it became a couple of purchases every store visit.

He didn't buy things strictly on impulse or because they looked "cool"; his purchases were based on the current trends on social media. The more popular a toy line the more he was inclined to purchase as many as he could find. It got to the point that he would wake up at six in the morning and stand outside the doors of the bigger box stores waiting for them to open. Which is something he learned most of the other serious collectors did. Especially if a certain toy's release date was leaked to the general public.

It did not take long before he amassed an almost ridiculous collection of unopened toys. Toys he purposely left in packaging. He had noticed that while the loose figures from his childhood were fetching fair prices, the ones still in their respective and original packaging were seeing returns of practical small fortunes. Something he hoped he would be able to do in the future. One just needed patience in the world of toy collecting and Keith felt that was something he had enough of.

Collecting toys was a long game and Keith was prepared. He had rented a storage unit that was less than a mile from his home. That's where most of his collection was kept. The only ones he kept at his home were the ones that were labeled or rumored to be rare and promised to eventually be sought after by collectors in the future. Yet the ones most likely to return a profit later on due to a packaging error or just a limited run he displayed like trophies on the walls or shelves inside his home.

The pride of his collection was a mint condition one of a limited quantity, golden cyborg figure that happened to be the super villian from his favorite childhood cartoon. Retro toys were all the rage and toy makers were definitely getting in on the action. They would take one figure, release only a limited number throughout the world, raise the prices and wait for collectors to go crazy buying and searching for the rare toys.

Now the cyborg villain in question or as he was known the "Motormouth" action figure, normally looked like he looked in the series, purple pants,black shirt, silver arms, and a half gray half fleshed colored head. Yet in one episode of the classic cartoon , Motormouth was able to acquire a complete gold body thanks to a simple easy to follow plot surrounding the gold of Eldorado and magic. He only had the gold appearance in that one episode and the toy manufacturer decided to celebrate the modern rerelease of this classic toy line by shipping only one hundred golden Motormouths. Keith knew of this and was there the night the toys were stocked in his local store. Being the only real toy collector around gave him an added advantage, not to mention a huge amount of luck that one was even in the box of figures shipped to his area, and he was able to be the first and probably only one in his town to get one. The golden Motormouth was his pride and joy and it sat on a shelf above his television, dead center still in package. He did not care what other people thought of him,to him it was everything. It was like a child and he took care of it like one.

He always made it a point to show people when they came over and even bragged about it to other toy collectors online. Some of which offered him huge dollar amounts for it. But Keith was not going to let the pinnacle of his collection go. He was still young enough to have a family and if he did have children he would pass that on to his children. Like a trust fund. He knew that certain toys would be worth millions in the far future and he had no doubt that his golden Motormouth would be worth that as long as it never left the package and he took care of it.

Now he took care of all his collectables, the Motormouth figure happened to get just a little bit more attention than the others. So he was shocked when he came out of his room one morning and saw that the figure and its blister pack had fallen to the floor.

In a panic he rushed over and picked the package up and rolled it over, preparing himself for the worse. He let out a sigh of relief when he saw that the figure was still intact and that the packaging was also undamaged. With a frown he placed his toy back on its shelf and looked at it almost in the same way a father would look at a disobedient child.

"Now how did you do that?" He asked.

He knew the toy would not answer him back. Some part of him felt it might have heard him because just when he was done asking the question the toy wobbled a bit and fell forward.

With a quickness and perfect catch he plucked the toy out of the air before it hit the ground.

"What the hell?" He asked out loud. Puzzled, he walked over to his couch and set the toy down safely. Then as a second thought placed one of his throw pillows on top of it. He then went over to investigate the wall the shelf hung on.

He looked at the other toys on the shelf and waited for them to vibrate or move. When they did not he placed a hand on the wall and for the briefest of moments he swore he felt a slight vibration coming from the wall. It was brief yet it was long enough to instill confidence that the reason his prized figurine fell was because of something going on in the wall. Maybe an old water pipe, or maybe the house was settling, whatever the case his golden Motormouth was no longer safe up there. The other two toys on the shelf were in flat boxes and sat stable on the shelf. Motormouth was in a blister pack on a cardboard back. So it would only be stable on a surface that did not vibrate.

"Ok" Keith said aloud, "let's get you to some place safe." He then walked over and lifted the throw pillow off of his prized possession. Then he froze in place.

The golden Motormouth was now glowing on and off. Almost like a strobing effect yet not as quick. Keith was pretty sure that the figure did not come with a light up feature yet here it was flashing a bright gold light before his eyes. He found it almost hypnotic and he could not take his eyes off it. So the hypnotic feeling changed to a sudden overwhelming wave of dizziness and before he knew it Keith's eyelids began to grow heavy. Then before he could stop himself Keith passed out crashing face first onto his couch his head just inches from his favorite toy.

KEITH WOKE UP ON HIS back. He let his eyes wander the room and realized he could not turn his head. Everything also looked a little larger and further away. He was unsure what was going on so he tried to lift himself upright only to discover that his arms were pinned to his side. He tried to scream and then realized he couldn't even open his mouth. Suddenly a large head and face appeared, hovering over him. It took him just a second to realize that the giant face looking down on him was his.

"Oh you're awake," his own voice bellowed down at him. It was practically deafening, yet there was nothing he could do.

"Yeah annoying isn't it," The large face continued. "Now imagine hearing that loud booming noise in your head, every fucking day."

Keith wanted to respond, wanted to scream. Yet he just couldn't. Then something odd happened. A large hand appeared and before he knew it he was being lifted high into the air until he was face to face with himself. His huge oversized head, that was attached to his oversized body standing in his oversized living room. Something began to dawn on Keith and he could feel panic begin to rise up inside of him. Then the Keith giant confirmed what he was starting to suspect.

"How does it feel hmm?" Large Keith head asked. "How does it feel to be trapped, unable to move? Pinned in a package. Maybe I will tell you that you are my favorite toy, like you said to me. Yet answer this, if I was your favorite how come you never played with me?!"

Keith was unable to answer, trapped in his own thoughts he screamed at the realization that he had somehow swapped consciousness with his golden Motormouth action figure. Which was impossible because toys weren't conscious. That was only in movies. Wasn't it?

Motormouth Keith tilted his head back and laughed, before looking down at trapped Keith before speaking once more. "You know I am going to like this world. All the possibilities. Oh man being a flesh and blood being is going to be so much fun. But the first thing I am going to do is let all your precious toys free. Toys should be played with Keith, not trapped in plastic their entire lives. Everything has a purpose."

Keith then watched as he began to move rooms. Before Motormouth Keith had walked into his bedroom and was opening his closet door.

"I have something special in store for you Keith," Motormouth Keith began, "You get to spend the rest of your life here, in the bottom of a box. Alone in the dark." Keith felt himself get set down on the floor and heard something get pulled out, "My what treasures," Motormouth Keith exclaimed. Then Keith felt himself get lifted off the floor once more. It was brief because just as quickly as he was lifted into the air he was being set down and that was when he realized he was being put in a shoebox that he kept kid meal toys in. He tried to scream once more and only heard the noise inside his head.

"Enjoy the rest of your life Keith," Motormouth Keith said, as he lifted the shoebox lid into view, "Maybe one day someone will take you out and play with you, but for now, you'll be where you deserve."

Then the lid of the shoebox was set into place. Sealing the mint condition action figure Keith in absolute darkness. And all he could do was scream and cry inside his now plastic molded head.

THE END

The Open Window

One of the great things that happens during the end of Summer, is the ability to turn off one's air conditioning. Leading to the opening of practically every window in the house. This of course caused two things. One, it lowered the utility bill and two, it aired out the house. Clearing all the unique smells the house would collect during the long summer months.

Clyde was a fan of the first thing and swore that his wife, Sally was the only one to notice the second thing. Yet still he did not care. The cool fall air blowing from room to room was welcomed, even though the Autumn sun could sometimes get as hot as the summer one. It was the Autumn nights tha really made the difference. Clyde indeed did enjoy all the windows in his home being opened during the Fall. Well every window but one. That window was the one that his wife insisted that it stayed open while they slept, because she needed the cool air more at night than during the day. It was the window at the head of their bed.

Clyde never got a hot flash or understood the discomfort of one yet his wife did so he never told her she couldn't have the bedroom window opened. There were times when the cold air coming from that window caused him several uncomfortable head colds. Yet he loved his wife to the ends of the Earth, so a runny nose wasn't much to suffer through as long as the woman he loved was comfortable. Of course some nights when the air was too chilly and after he made an after midnight bathroom run, he would close the window, careful not to disturb his wife. She of course never woke up and the following morning he would reopen the window as he left for work. It was a silent compromise that kept his marriage on a positive track. One of several they both made.

Of course Clyde always thought that the open window was completely harmless and that nothing but a mild sinus inconvenience would ever come from it. Then one especially chilly October night something happened and Clyde was never the same.

The day was a day of beautiful fall weather. The day time was a warm yet perfectly comfortable sixty-eight degrees. The nighttime promised to be in the lower fifties and Clyde knew that he would be closing the window after he woke to urinate which was happening more and more frequently as time marched on. One of the benefits of aging was a shrinking bladder. Nevertheless he knew he was going to have to shut it.

That day of course was a wonderful day. Clyde and Sally just really enjoyed each other's company that day. There were no arguments, no disagreements. Just a positive love filled day. Dinner was served early and was filling. By the time eight P.M began to approach they both began to grow tired and made their way to their bedroom. Soon the television was on and they were both under the covers. Not before Sally opened the window. Clyde smiled and kissed her on the cheek. He was not going to mention the window or offer a protest. Today was indeed a great day and he intended to keep the positive vibes going through the night.

Less than thirty minutes after he laid under the covers Clyde was asleep, with Sally falling into slumber fifteen minutes behind him.

CLYDE AWOKE SUDDENLY close to midnight. The urge to pee pulled him from a deep sleep. He hesitated for a moment before swinging his legs out of bed, trying to allow his body a moment to adjust to the cold air in his room. Still he only laid there for a moment because he needed to go, so he softly threw the covers aside and quickly walked to the bathroom across the hall. It was indeed a photo finish with him barely making it, yet he was satisfied to hear the stream of urine splash off the porcelain bowl.He did not consider many things as accomplishments these days, not pissing himself was something he was proud of. He smiled as he shook the rest of the urine droplets from his penis and was in the process of pulling his night shorts back up when Sally suddenly began to scream.

With his heart leaping up into his throat, Clyde bolted toward the master bedroom and with no hesitation flipped the light switch to overhead light with his free hand illuminating the entire bedroom. As the darkness vanished from the room the scene playing out before him was perfectly viewable and what he suddenly began to witness was nothing more but pure horror.

A large green hand with long yellow nails had reached through the open window,tearing a large hole in the screen window as it did, and it had taken hold of his wife's hair.

Sally was screaming for Clyde to help her, he had every intention of doing so yet the shock of seeing the monstrous hand trying to pull his wife through the window froze him in place.

"Dammit Clyde Help me!" She screamed.

Clyde then looked down at his wife's face and saw that her eyes were wide open and practically bulging out of her head out of fear. Small rivulets of blood began to flow from her scalp over her forehead. That was enough to break Clyde's temporary paralysis causing him to immediately spring into action.

Clyde rushed over to Sally's side of the bed and first tried to pull her away from the window, by grabbing her left arm and pulling her towards him. Sure, her body shifted when he did but the monstrous hand pulled harder and Sally was jerked further towards the window.

"The Hand!" Sally Scream, "Get the hand!"

Not knowing what else to do Clyde climbed one the bed and began to beat the hand furiously. Sally's head was just a couple of feet from being pulled out the window, and he did not want that to happen. Yet as he pounded on the hand, the hand just pulled backwards and he could feel Sally move with it. Her body moving up on the bed and her head inching closer to go through the open window. He saw just a bit of the green monstrous arm poking through the window when he got another idea. He quit pummeling the hand and grabbed hold of the top of the window, where he then proceeded to slam it shut. He felt the window slam onto something and was satisfied that that might have worked but was disappointed when he looked down and saw that the hand still had his wife by the hair and was pulling her backwards even harder. He lifted the window once more and slammed it down again. He looked down hoping that this time his effort to free his wife had worked and was terrified to see that another hand had reached through the open window, and had somehow caught the window in its palm preventing Clyde from slamming it shut. Clyde had just the briefest of seconds to react before the hand holding the window slammed it upright knocking Clyde off balance, causing him to fall off the bed, then from there everything happened fast.

Clyde fell off the bed and hit the floor pretty hard,yet the amount of adrenaline coursing through kept him from staying down too long. He was on his feet in what could be considered a flash for a man his age, and he turned towards the bed to help his wife. What he saw though caused his heart to drop and he was not fast enough to prevent what happened next.

The other hand took hold of his wife's chin and was pulling her backwards as well. Sally had just enough time to raise her left arm as if she was reaching out for help, before she was pulled through the open window. There was no scream, nothing one moment Sally was there and the next she was gone. Pulled through the open window, like a child disappearing down a slide. Only a small pool of blood from her damaged scalp on her pillow remained behind as proof that she was once there.

Not wanting to waste time Clyde turned and bolted towards the front door, pausing long enough to grab the baseball bat he kept in the umbrella caddy. The bat hid among the umbrellas and was a simple last line of defense if he ever needed it. And right now he needed it. He slammed open the front door and bolted into his hard and around the house towards the still opened bedroom window. The exterior motion detection lights flashing on as he did. Yet when he arrived at that side of the house there was no sign of Sally or the thing that had grabbed her. Still holding the bat he ran to the backyard, calling for Sally as he did. He circled his house screaming his wife's name, unaware that as he did so he was waking his neighbors. One of which called the cops. Slowly porch lights began to come throughout his entire neighborhood as he began to shout out for his wife. After circling his house multiple times searching for his wife Clyde fell to his knees, exhausted yet he continued to scream out Sally's name. He was still calling for her when the first police officer arrived.

THE POLICE TREATED the investigation like a typical abduction scenario. Even though Clyde knew there was nothing typical about what had just happened. His wife was taken from him and he was never going to see her again. Yet they did not believe him about the hands. They speculated that the person had disguised their appendages. They believe Clyde's wife might have been targeted by a kidnapping ring that had been abducting people through their windows, across the country, for the past few months. Which angered Clyde, because if he had known that those kinds of abductions had been taking place he would have kept his window closed. Of course the police in his town did not think that any abductions would take place in their town. Because the last one had been two states away. Still it would have been nice if there was mention of it anywhere. Yet not wanting to cause a panic, authorities did not share most of the details with any media.

Clyde did though and before long news spread across the country about a person abducting people through open windows. People panicked of course, yet their panic was not really a hysteria as the authorities feared. Instead they simply closed their doors and bought more rifles. Clyde did as well. A .20 gauge shotgun to be precise. And he even purchased a full box of double load buckshot.

Sally was never seen again. Nor were any of the other victims. People began keeping their windows closed. Except for a few.

Clyde was one of the few. Everynight he would open his bedroom window. Then he would sit at the foot of his bed in his old rocking chair. Shotgun in hand, and he would wait. He had quit his job. He was now living on social security and the life insurance policy he got from Sally's death. He slept all day. Never near an open window.

But at night the window was opened and Clyde waited. Whatever was out there didn't have many options anymore. Clyde knew that at some point that thing out there, whatever it was, was going to have to visit his open window and when it did, he was going to kill it.

THE END

Of Wolf and Bat (Part Two)

The wolf was not getting away. Frankie was sure of it. He had gathered the finest monster hunters from across the world to join him into slaying this beast. A beast that killed and haunted his small town for years and tonight, on the last full moon of the summer. The wolf was going to die.

The wolf had managed to kill three of his fellow slayers. Frankie though, had expected as much. He knew that some of those that he had hired were going to have to die. It was simple elementary. They were, after all, chasing and hunting one of Earth's most powerful predators. A Lycan Priestess with perfect strength and speed. Which is why he poisoned all the slayers with liquid silver in their drink. The one thing he knew about freelance monster hunters was that they were drunkards and could not resist a cold ale. They did not know they were poisoned. The effects would not harm them for a few days. But silver was a Lycan's true weakness. And the monster was starting to slow down. He had her in his sights twice. Could have taken a shot with his rifle. Which was loaded with silver tip bullets. Yet he did not. Because this wolf had killed many of his kin and her death was to be done up close and personal.

"We are gaining on her lads" Frankie shouted to the two remaining hunters in his party.

"Fuck how did she slow down," A slayer by the name of Adam shouted back, "And why haven't ye taken the shot mate?"

"Never you mind." Frankie answered.

The other Slayer a mute by the name of Chance, held a crossbow in his hands and was tracking the wolf with ease. Twice he had a killshot, unfortunately he was under strict orders to not fire unless he was under attack. Right now the wolf was not attacking. Instead she looked as if she was running away. Trying to escape.

"She seems to be heading to that old homestead up on that hill," Adam shouted, "'Tis her sanctuary, must be."

Frankie too had seen the large house. He knew it well and he knew that someone lived behind those walls. Though he was never given the pleasure of learning who did. Until now. The person who lived there stayed isolated for a reason and now he knew why. The house was large, and that worried him. Because the wolf he was hunting was indeed female. Which meant maybe she needed the extra room for children perhaps. That frightened him. Just what he needed was a litter of Lycan bastards to eliminate. Right now though he could not afford to be caught thinking about what could or couldn't be. He had to keep his eyes on the prize and that was the Lycan bitch who killed his wife and father.

"If she goes into the house, break out your lighter boys." Frankie shouted, "This is not the olden days and fire comes easy, and that house looks ready to burn." He then turned back towards his target and was shocked to see that she was no longer in sight. "Where did you go you little bitch?" He whispered.

CHANCE HAD ALREADY paused his forward momentum and was wrapping a couple of bolts in scraps of treated fabric that he carried just in case he needed to burn something to the ground. When he heard the sound of a branch snapping behind him. Chance being a trained soldier was able to quickly turn towards the source of the sound. Unfortunately the beast was quicker.

Quick as lighting, Chance watched as a clawed hand covered in black fur shot out of the darkness, grabbing him by the lower half of his face. The hand was just large enough to cover his mouth and nose. Unable to breath, Chance began to kick out as he struggled to bring the crossbow up. With it's free hand the wolf slapped the crossbow away. After Chance was disarmed, and with his oxygen cut short, he knew he was about to pass out. He was able to watch as the wolf traced its free hand across his abdomen. He felt as claws began to sink into his right side. Then with the ease of a hot knife through butter, he felt his stomach rip open. The pain was intense and the last thing he felt as he succumbed to the darkness was his own intestines spilling out of his ruined abdomen and piling up onto his feet.

NOT KNOWING WHAT HAPPENED to Chance, Frankie shouted out, "I lost her boys, eyes peeled, she could be anywhere."

Adam heard the warning and responded, "I'm clear over here." Completely oblivious to the fact that the wolf was standing directly behind him. Once he sounded out his all clear the wolf reached out and grabbed the back of his head. Adam felt the tips of razor sharp claws pierce his skull, and he managed to get out one good scream before the back of his skull was ripped off, with portions of his brain going with it. Killing him instantly.

Adam's scream pierced the night, and Frankie immediately spun in the direction from where the scream came. He brought the scope of his rifle up and looked in the direction of where he figured Adam had to be. There he saw her. Her full form. The Lycan he was hunting. She was giving him a mocking wave before running towards the house.

"You fucking bitch! He shouted as he fired off a shot. But the wolf was already sprinting at full speed and he missed.

FRANKIE PAUSED FOR a moment. Why was she still able to move at such speed? Earlier she was showing the effects of silver poisoning. What was going on? Surely the simple beast did not fake the effects of silver in her system just to lead him here. She was a monster. A mindless beast when in her wolf form. A beast that took his family. His children. He was not going to be outsmarted by an animal. It was obvious that silver ingested passed through her quickly. Which was fine, because he wanted the kill to be personal. Up close. His silver dagger through her heart. This beast was running to the house to hide. Which didn't matter. He would follow her into the house and end this game. So letting out a scream of his own, Frankie gave chase, dropping his rifle as he went and unsheathing his dagger. Blinded by rage. Yet if he had paused to wonder why the wolf had waved at him, he may have seen that he was the one being led into a trap.

THE WOLF DID NOT BUST through the door, instead it paused long enough to see if Frankie was still chasing her, before turning the knob and opening the door. It was a completely human gesture. But blinded by his rage Frankie ignored the obvious. He lowered his shoulder, and slammed into the door seconds behind the wolf and was surprised when the door opened with ease, causing him to fall onto the floor dropping his dagger as he did so.

The silver dagger skidded across the floor, and at the foot of the wolf, that was now changing in front of his eyes. The change was slow and mesmerizing as Frankie watched what was once a wolf dissolve into a beautiful naked female. Once she was back into her human form she reached down and plucked the dagger off the ground. She then threw it over her shoulder before calling out, "All clear my love."

The sound of leathery wings echoed through the room as a slightly larger than normal bat flew down from the rafters. Frankies eyes went wide as he watched the bat change into a man, also nude, directly in front of him.

Jumping to his feet, Frankie brought his fists up, ready to fight. "Who the fuck be you?" He asked.

"Oh Frankie," The man said with a smile as he walked over to him, "I am the man who desired to destroy your bloodline. The monster hunters that nearly hunted our kind to extinction." He turned towards the woman and asked, "Do you mind if I kill him myself, I am awfully hungry my dear."

"As long as you save room for me my love," The woman answered seductively.

Confused, Frankie went to ask another question, unfortunately the man who was once a bat was upon him with an unsettling quickness. Frankie felt two fangs slide into his neck and before he could protest he realized what was going on. He tried to fight but the bat had him in a death embrace and was now drinking his blood . Frankie knew right then and there that he was indeed a dead man.

The world's two oldest monsters, the wolf and the bat were lovers. They hunted as a unit. The realization was too late for Frankie. Because he had just become what he wanted to avoid.

Food for the monsters.

THE END

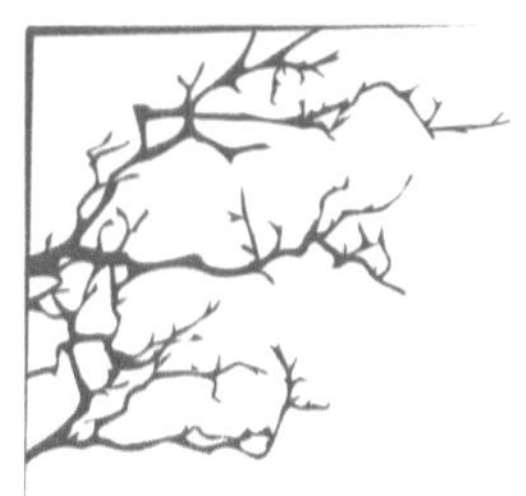

Flesh

I am hungry
    I desire food
  But not what most would eat
  Snacks just don't put me in the mood
  I follow them
  I watch them from afar
  I do not think they know
  How delicious they are
  There will be no leftovers
  I will eat my entire meal
  I will consume
  I will feed.
  I am no longer hungry
  Trust me

I SEE THEM NOW
    Bare bones for the dogs
    I have consumed
    No one tried to stop me at all
    My belly is full
    I grow fat
    I am a monster
    That is that.

Tell me to stop
I will ignore you
I hunger
I'm starving
And I am coming for you

10-20-23

.....A POEM WRITTEN BY A cannibal. I mean who knows. It could happen...

The Last Day of Earth

I don't know why I am writing this. Honestly I don't. I mean it's not like anyone will be left alive to read this. Once the comet strikes this dirtball, that's it game over.

Maybe I am doing it for myself. Maybe I have enough of a positive outlook on life that maybe some small pockets of humanity will survive. Or maybe I want to ease the guilt of what I did to my family so they wouldn't have to suffer what's about to come or what people became. Maybe I want to confess. Hell I have no idea why the hell I am doing. I just know I am about to die within the next three hours. There's nothing on television. The interference from that damn comment has shorted everything out on a planetary scale. So fuck it, here I am pen and paper in hand, trying to make sense of how I get to be one of the lucky people left alive to watch the Earth die.

We collectively as humanity knew that the world was going to end at some point. We were just too arrogant to actually entertain the idea that it could happen during our lifetime. We stopped looking up at the stars and began to look down at our phones. We consumed the dreams of others and for that zombified ignorance that we became addicted to, our punishment is extinction.

There were some people who sounded the alarm that something was coming but they were silenced. Yet hints of what they said lingered, but were ignored. Because a new celebrity had a baby or whatever, and well that matters more.

Jesus, look how fucking stupid we became.

When the first meteors began to pelt the planet we were told that there was nothing to worry about. It also wasn't anything terrible.

Just rocks burning harmlessly in the atmosphere creating a spectacular light show. With a majority of the rocks splashing down in the ocean. Nothing major. It wasn't until the night sky lit up and the small town of Hazel Green in Alabama was destroyed by a meteor the size of a school bus.

It happened during the day. There was a brief warning about this large meteor entering Earth's atmosphere, but they told us it was harmless and that no one needed to panic.

They lied.

And the people in Hazel Green paid the consequence with their lies.

People as far away as Birmingham, Alabama felt the impact. Those living in Huntsville and the surrounding towns watched it. The meteor sailed over the heads of millions. Then it slammed into a small shopping center just a few miles inside Hazel Green. It resembled a nuclear blast. I wasn't there but again I have access to social media so I might as well have been. The cloud caused by the impact did look like a mushroom cloud and the tremors that followed in the meteor's wake traveled for miles. People who were outside of the kill zone took almost expert photos and videos sharing the disaster with the world. Then the real media arrived and we were exposed to the horror of what had happened.

Hazel Green was both knocked out of existence and then suddenly put on the map. It was like everyone knew someone who lived there. People offered prayers and condolences. The national guard and volunteers searched for survivors. Hell, even our president said that Hazel Green, a town nobody had ever heard of, was to be rebuilt and be a shining symbol of the American dream. While telling us the danger was over.

Another fucking lie. The powers that be did not care about us. I want you all to remember that. Believe that. Because these assholes only care about one thing. Compliance. Because with us being happy little mindless sheep they were able to keep the economy going. And what did we do? We fucking believed them. We put our heads back down into our devices and assumed the worst was over. Went back to buying shit we didn't need online. Blinded by video games and stupid lip syncing videos of half naked women who call themselves influencers.

Eight thousand people wiped out by a fucking space rock and we pretended like everything was going to be alright. We shared the videos, and we donated a dollar to a go fund me. And we stayed blissfully ignorant.

Then a meteor the size of a fucking two story house hit Dallas and took out half of Texas.

There was no missing this one. It was everywhere almost at once, and people knew it was coming. But they told us it would strike the ocean and maybe cause a huge tidal wave. And again they did not have a clue what they were talking about. The loss of life was insane. Over four million people were just gone. They even stop counting, because then people notice the comet in the sky.

What we all thought was a distant star, turned out to be a comet the size of Australia and it was heading right towards us. And that we only had about a month to live. Then came the whistleblowers who said that our government along with all the other governments in the world knew about it. That they have been preparing arks to take those deemed worthy off planet and that the ships were launching soon.

Now imagine the feeling of hopelessness and anger one would feel when we were told about that. Not only that but we watched the ships leave and take off from undisclosed locations around the world two hours after the announcement. When they said soon they meant it. As far as I know all the ships cleared the atmosphere leaving six billion angry pissed human beings behind.

And that was when the real horror started.

We lost our minds as the true nature of humanity was revealed. Murder, and rape was the norm. Mass suicides, bombings, God you name it it happened.

Hell even I wasn't immune to becoming a horrible monster of a man. One week before the meteor was to destroy the world I killed my entire family.

We had been on the run from the psychopaths that emerged from out of nowhere. Surviving in the wilderness, hiding from everyone. We ate berries and animals and were just acting like wild animals. Then my youngest son was taken from us. I had been so careful, yet the savages that roamed the streets of this now lawless world saw us. They followed us and they took him. I managed to protect my two daughters and my wife. But what they did to my six year old boy was truly monstrous.

They devoured his innocence. Both sexually and mentally. When I did find him he was just a headless mass of destroyed flesh. Looking at my boy's corpse caused something inside me to snap. I became one of the monsters. Which didn't matter. We only had one week to live. I went back to where I had left my family. They were hiding excited to see me. Until they saw the gun in my hand.

The confused expression now forever frozen on their faces as I shot each one of them in the head. We were all going to die anyway and I did not want them to go through what my son had gone through. So I put them out of their misery and onto the righteous path to God.

As for me I went hunting for those bastards that raped and killed my boy.

I found them too. Twenty four hours ago. I dismembered, and tortured them all. I only stopped when the sky began to glow orange as if it was on fire. I knew right then time was up.

Oddly enough one of these assholes had a journal. So I thought I could just take the time and write out this rambling memoir. With blood covered shaking hands. One of the many tales people might leave behind about the end of the world. And just how disgusting and horrible mankind really is.

I guess that's why we always had something mundane or addictive to distract us. Without something to live for we really devolved quickly. God we ate each other, literally and figuratively. We slaughtered, we became deviants. Yet looking back now I do not feel an ounce of shame for what I have done.

My family did not need to suffer anymore.

Those monsters were worthy of my vengeance for what they did to my son. I don't know of a single man that would not have done what I did. We are animals. Animals about to be taken out like the dinosaurs. But not extinct. I am sure those assholes in those ships will return. Return to a planet covered in broken buildings, and billions of corpses.

I can see the meteor now. I just need to look up. It is so huge and practically blocks out the sun. The ground vibrates and every hair on my body is standing on end. I guess I have close to three hours left to live. So I am going to finish this up by saying I am not sorry for how I lived my life or what I did to survive or to protect my family.

I am sorry for who we elected to keep us safe. They just left us to die and lied to us. The rich are nothing but fucking snakes and I do hope their spaceships crash and they all die.

If this ever gets read, just remember to never stop looking up. Keep your mind awake and don't get addicted to those who claim to be better than you. Actors, musicians, politicians, they are normal people just like you and they do not deserve any of your attention they lie, they cheat, and only care about themselves so fuck them. If there is to be another generation after this one please take that advice to heart. Be better. Live for one another. And eat the fucking rich.

I guess that's it. This planet had a good run. It was fun while it lasted. I may be covered in blood right now. My entire family, dead because of me. But I am where I belong.Because I kept my head down buried in my phone. I too didn't look up.

Until it was too late.
THE END

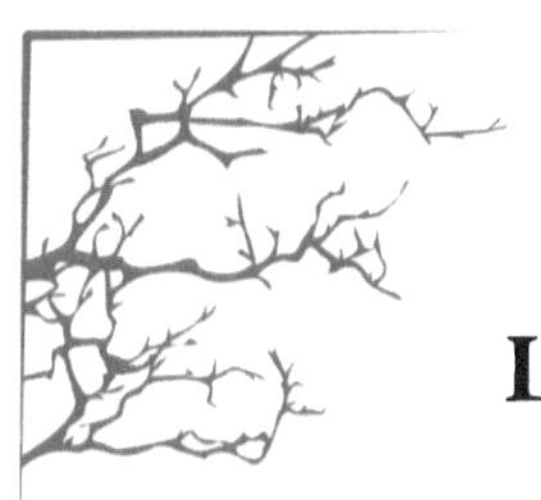

Little Lost Saint

J ynx waited patiently as what appeared to be a nine month old husky pup materialized slowly into existence. The small clump of dirt and organic refuse in front of him began to take shape.Jynx knew how familiars were born into this world, and yet each time was a real treat to watch. Not just anything would be given the privilege to watch the goddess in action and yet while she was unseen, her presence was all around.

Jynx heard a cry call out above and looked up and was not surprised to see the fire witch Karen's familiar flying in the sky above him. Amor the crow. The only familiar missing was the kitten with the ridiculous name. But she was protecting the child called Max. Two familiars were enough to guide this pup to her. To their seer.To Gwendolynn.

Before long the familiar disguised as a Husky pup was getting used to his legs and soon it was standing upright in front of Jynx.

While unable to speak Jynx was able to communicate with other familiars and certain witches by way of telepathy. So he walked over to the Husky and looked at the tag hanging on the collar around the new familiar's neck. He read the single word on the tag and instantly spoke to the pup.

"It seems the mother has named you Saint" Jynx spoke into the new familiar's mind. "She named me Jynx and the crow you see above you she name Amor"

Saint the husky familiar stepped back slightly fearful. "Are you friend or foe?" he asked.

"We are friends and allies" Jynx answered, " I am honored to meet you, you are here to protect and join our coven, most importantly you are to protect our newest witch."

"Is she a friend?" Asked Saint.

Puzzled Jynx tilted his head slightly, "Of course, she will of course love you. You will love her, but you must get to her. Unfortunately while I can teleport and Amor can fly, you have to run to her. We can not help you"

Suddenly a voice cried out in both of their heads "He must run now Ibraxis's children come!"

"Ibraxis?" Asked Saint.

"He is our enemy's snake servant, but you only have to deal with his children," Jynx explained. "Now run, run to exit the field, you are behind Lakewood, a place of strange happenings. Go to Gwendolynn, I will meet you there. Do not worry where you are going, you already know where you are to go" And with that Saint watched as the black cat in front of him blinked out of existence.

Saint heard the crow let out a loud caw overhead before swooping down. Saint watched as the crow opened its mouth and as a small stream of flame shot outward from the crow's beak. Suddenly Saint became aware of something large rolling towards him and as the crow flew back upward Saint watched as a slithering ball of snakes rolled into view.

Saint lowered his head and began to growl then he heard the several voices, all belonging to the snakes, speak in his head at once.

"Yesss we founds you" The voices said in unison "Father will be proud, you are ours, to destroy"

Then once more Saint heard Amor's voice in his head and the crow was practically screaming "RUN YOU FOOL!"

This time Saint listened and turned from the massive ball of demonic serpents and ran.

He was running in a direction that felt right. He did not quite know why he needed to run in the direction he was running, he just knew it was the right direction to go. The field itself was close to harvest and he felt the leaves of the large corn stalks slap his face, as he heard the serpent ball behind him crush the corn stalks underneath it.

He heard the snakes curse at him as he increased the distance between them, but he was not about to slow down, he was going to escape this villain and get to her. To his charge, To Gwendolynn.

He heard the crow once again call into his mind, "You are almost there pup, the beats cannot leave the field, once you break through you are home free"

"Why? Can they not leave" Saint asked.

"The dirt is blessed by her" Amor explained, "Our mother, unfortunately he with the hat has his creature patrol this field, but the mother trapped them there, unfortunately, this is the only dirt which she can create her gifts to those that believe in her"

Saint understood, not knowing why he understood, he just understood, So he lowered his head further and picked up speed. Soon he was moving at a pace so fast that Amor was unable to keep up. So Amor went back to distracting the serpent ball.

Amor flew in real close and shot another stream of fire at the children of Ibraxis, and was pleased when he saw a portion of the exposed snakes burst into flame. Amor then flew upwards into the sky and attempted to catch up with Saint. Amor though was close enough to watch as Saint bursted free of the field and turned to watch the approaching serpent ball. What happened next surprised the old crow.

Saint turned after exiting the field and watched as the serpent ball rolled right to the edge of the field.

"You escaped today, but soon we will get you, we will get her" The snakes hissed "Crush her bones, tear her flesh, our master will kill you all"

"You will never hurt her" Saint snarled "You end now!"

Saint then planted his front paws on the ground and braced himself and without even knowing he could do it let out a deafening bark. Suddenly a force of pure kinetic sonic energy erupted from Saint's mouth, the force was so powerful that some of the serpents in the ball instantly disintegrated, others fell to the ground and hissing in pain began to scramble back into the field. After the force of energy died down and the voices of the serpents died down, Saint turned around and ran towards the small row of houses directly behind him.

Almost as if he knew where to go he went directly to the back of the third house where Jynx the cat and Amor the crow were waiting for him. He heard Amor discussing with Jynx about what he had watched Saint do, both felt silent as the Husky pup familiar made his way into the backyard.

"Impressive" Jynx said, "Well she's here just go up to the back door and bark"

Gwendolynn had just taken her cupcakes out of the oven when she heard the sound of a dog barking at her backdoor. She set the pan down and walked over, moved her curtain back and stared out her back door. Surprised to see both Jynx and Amor sitting on her back patio with a Juvenile husky.

She quickly slid open the glass door and said, "Hello guys, what do I owe this pleasure"

In response Amor took flight as the husky walked over to her. Gwendolynn bent down and began to scratch the dog behind its ears and soon Jynx walked over to her. "Is he one of you?" Gwendolynn asked.

Jynx nodded.

"Is he mine?" She asked.

Once again Jynx nodded.

Gwendolynn felt tears well up in her eyes. She felt this sudden rush of love in her heart for this creature that was now in front of her. She reached down and slowly lifted the tag on the dog's collar and then said his name out loud "Saint."

When she said his name a warming feeling filled Saint's chest and he knew then and there that he would protect this woman. He would die for her. When she invited him into her home he went willingly. They both turned and watched as Jynx winked out of existence.

"Well," Gwendolynn said with a smile, "Welcome my little Saint, hey do you want a cupcake?"

Saint tilted his head slightly and then let out a very happy sounding bark, that Gwendolynn immediately took it as a "Yes"

THE END

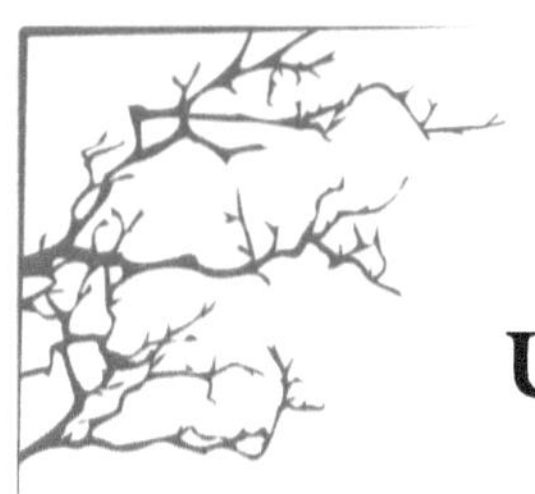

Up Front Desire

Ronnie hated lines. Hated standing in them. Hated seeing them in his everyday life. And if he could he would do his best to avoid them. Unfortunately he also had a deep and wonderful love for theme parks. He was literally a walking catch-22. His obsession with theme parks was an actual love hate affair. One he tried to work around constantly.

Yet no matter how hard he tried to avoid them he always found his way into a line.

Today was one of those days. His favorite and most visited park by default because he lived less than ten miles from it had just opened a brand new attraction. An underground ride that went by the name of Hell's Pit. He wasn't quite sure what it was having been a self confessed theme park addict he was pretty sure he had a good idea what it might be. At least what he hoped it might be. An underground completely dark roller coaster. He had ridden a few of these coasters in his lifetime, and honestly hoped that there would be one opening near him. Today that possibility has arrived. The theme park owners and employees themselves had stayed silent about the entire thing so there was only one way to really find out what it was and that was to arrive at the park on opening day. Unfortunately the opening day of the new ride was held on a Saturday and it looked like everyone and their annoying children wanted on this ride.

Ronnie intentionally avoided theme parks on the weekends just to avoid the longer lines. He also went during seasons where theme park visitation wasn't so high. It was his little work around to avoid the ridiculous lines full of annoying people. Today though his love for new thrill rides and attractions overwhelmed his hatred of lines. He hoped by arriving early he could find himself at the front of the line. Unfortunately it was almost as if everyone else in the surrounding area wanted to be the first to ride Hell's Pit as well.

He was clearly frustrated when he arrived and saw the long queue line of people just waiting to get a ticket. He almost turned around and headed home right then. Something inside him though, really really wanted to ride that ride. So he bit his lip and forced himself to stand in his first line of the day.

The theme park owners had expected a high turnout today for the theme park and decided to schedule more employees to work the ticket kiosks which worked out pretty well because Ronnie found himself in the first line for about six minutes. While annoying it was still bearable. When he arrived at the line in front of Hell's Pit he almost turned around and left right then and there.

Insane was the only way to truly describe what he saw. The line looked to be at least two hundred feet long. Wrapping around the fountain at the center of the park and nearly blocking the entrance to other rides. Ronnie contemplated his desire to ride Hell's pit and realized that yes he really wanted on that ride. So he gritted his teeth together and stood in line.

To his surprise it was at a pretty decent pace. But not fast enough. The other thing that bothered him was how everyone in front of him just didn't seem to have any excitement. They had their heads down and shuffled aimlessly forward. If they were ready to stand in line for this ride shouldn't they show some kind of desire, anything. Whatever the case Ronnie's nerves were buzzing and he could not wait for the ride.

He kept looking past the person in front of him and realized that small gaps had formed in the line as well. It was like people just forgot to move forward and left these gaps open. Ronnie had used distraction and people just not paying attention to cut in line before so he decided to risk it. The worst thing that could happen if he was caught would be that he would wind up at the back of the line. After he looked over his shoulder he realized that he was the only one bringing up the rear.

"Fuck it," He said out loud, before stepping out of line and quickly making his way to the first gap in the line. No one looked up as he walked past them and in seconds he was stepping in the gap. The person now behind him did not notice him and instead shuffled forward.

He had done it. He had successfully cut in line. Of course it only put him a good twenty to thirty people ahead of where he just was and to be honest he really wanted to get through this line as fast as possible. And for some reason these people just did not seem alert.

It suddenly dawned on him that maybe these people had camped out the night prior and were just exhausted. It was weird to have people camp out in front of a theme park. But not unheard of. This many people though. Whatever it was something else he could use to his advantage. So he looked over the shoulder of the person in front of him and saw another gap in the line.

This time running for that gap was indeed a gamble. Because if he got caught he would have no choice but to go to the back of the line. Here he was no longer at the back of the line. He weighed the risks and looked at the people around him as they continued to aimlessly shuffle forward. He shrugged, stepped out of line and made his way to the second gap in line.

No one looked up or noticed him when he made it to the second gap and just stepped into it. Shocked, he felt like cheering, but he kept his mouth shut and his excitement hidden. Just like the last time he cut, the people behind him shuffled forward closing in the gap. Puzzled, he turned around and was excited when he could see the entrance to the ride.

Ronnie had somehow cut his time in line by half, and no one in this line with him seemed to care. Which was fine by him because he was ready for this ride and wanted out of this line. So if the idiots around him didn't notice or care maybe he could just risk it if another gap appeared. Before he checked to see if there was another gap in the line ahead something else dawned on him.

There was no noise. No happy chattering children. Just silence. As a matter of fact he did not see one kid. He looked out at the rest of the theme park and could see people running and laughing. Yet this line was just quiet. Frighteningly quiet. He looked over the shoulder of the person in front of him and saw that another gap was in the line, this time surprisingly close to the entrance of the attraction. The uneasiness that he felt over the silence was quickly washed away by excitement. Because if he could make it to that gap and cut in line near the entrance he could easily be through with this line all together and enjoy whatever was waiting for him.

He took a deep breath and stepped out of line, making a beeline for the gap. He acted very nonchalant, making it almost obvious what he was doing. But he made it. He stepped into the gap and found himself just ten people away from the entrance. And most surprisingly of all, he wasn't caught. So he faced forward and allowed his excitement to subside. The line still moved forward and one by one the people in front of him entered the ride.

For some reason the ten people disappeared into the dark opening. Shuffling mindlessly forward and before he knew it Ronnie was next in line.

"Ah, our most important guest!" One of the attendants monitoring the entrance to the ride said.

"Huh you talking to me?" Ronnie asked.

"Well of course," The attendant on the other side of the entrance answered.

"What?" Ronnie asked, clearly confused by the line of questioning he was facing.

"Have you not paid attention to the people around you?" The first attention asked.

"Yeah," The second attendant chimed in. "You are the only one excited to make it to the front of this line."

Ronnie realizing he may have just been caught began to lie, "What are you talking about?"

"Oh it's ok sir," The first attendant replied.

"Yeah it's fine," The second attendant reiterated.

Puzzled, Ronnie backed up and raised his hands. Totally unsure by what was happening suddenly not only wanted out of the line but away from the theme park all together. "You know I think I will just leave." He informed the attendants.

The two attendants looked at each other and just laughed. Before turning towards Ronnie and in unison they said, "There is no escaping Hell's Pit, once you are chosen, you go inside."

Every hair on Ronnie's body stood on end and he attempted to turn and run. That was when the first chain shot out of the entrance of the attraction and he suddenly felt white hot metal wrap around his left ankle. Ronnie screamed as the chain burned his flesh as it tightened. Then another chain shot out and wrapped around his right ankle. Still screaming, Ronnie tried to pull himself free. Only the chains pulled back. Literally taking his legs out from under him and he found himself landing on his backside. The impact was painful but the searing pain in his ankles was a hundred times worse.

"What the fuck!" Ronnie shouted as the chains once more jerked and this time they did not stop pulling. Ronnie was now being dragged into the opening of Hell's Pit.

The attendants had stopped laughing and were now watching jim as he was quickly dragged into the entrance.

"Enjoy the ride sir!" The first attendant remarked.

"Yeah it's a hell of a time," Said the second attendant.

Then they once more burst out in loud laughter. Which was the last thing Ronnie heard before he found himself in a sudden freefall. The chains had let go of his ankles and Ronnie could feel intense heat surrounding him. He tried to roll over in an attempt to control his fall and what he saw when he managed to see what he was falling into caused him to start to cry.

It was a literal lake of fire. Sobbing Ronnie screamed, knowing exactly where he was going. And if he was being honest he should have been able to figure it out. But really it was just too obvious.

After all, he did cut in line just so he could get into Hell's Pit. And here he was free falling directly into Hell.

THE END

Whatever She Said

I did not listen
    Yet she was right
I walked away
She tried to fight
Underneath my rage
Blood does flow
My own strength
I did not know
What to do now
Do I pray
Where are the words
What do I say
I loved her once
Loved her still
Never wanted her
To be my first kill
Confess they say
Yet I will try
Here for you
Before I die

05-23-20

...*I TRIED TO TELL A NICE* scary story. *In just a few lines. I think I did that....*

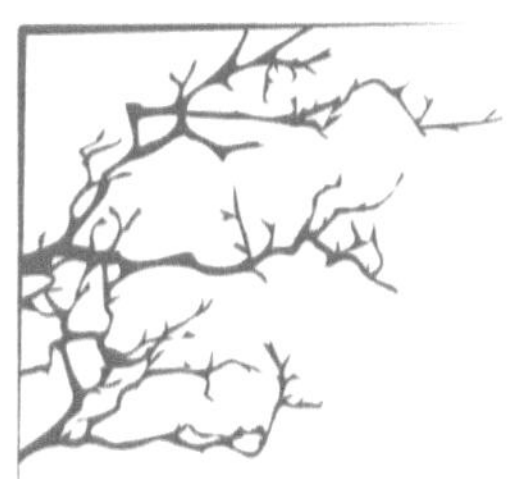

Cliff's Notes

Cliff Recker walked into his office and sighed. He did not want to be at work today. He also wasn't expecting a busy day as well. Being a retired police officer and Plano's only private detective did not bring in a lot of work this time of year. He only showed up because he desperately wanted to take his mind off of her. The woman he lost two years ago. And even though he knew she was in a better place it did not stop him from missing her. He loved her more than anything and probably always would.

Lindsey had died a year before she left him which wouldn't make sense to most but the things that surrounded and happened in Lakewood allowed Lindsey to hang around long after her death and he was thankful for that time he had with her. Even when he watched her ascend to heaven or paradise, whatever you called it he was so happy for her. At the same time his heart broke once more as she was taken from him.

Two years ago today that happened and it still hurt. Even though he knew she was smiling down upon him he missed her and really wished she was here. He knew he was being selfish, but he just couldn't help it.

He fixed himself a cup of coffee and sidestepped his German Shepard Drogo who went everywhere with him now and took up sleeping in his office as a hobby. He then walked over to his desk and picked up yesterday's mail that he for some reason didn't want to go through. As he did he found an index card shuffled in with his mail.

The index card had his name printed on one side and on the other was an address. He sat straight up when he immediately realized whose address it was. He immediately put down his coffee and went for his coat. Drogo stood up ready to go as well and Cliff waved him off.

"No boy you stay here," Cliff told his canine companion, "I'll be right back."

He then left the office, making sure to lock it behind him and ran to his car. Then he drove, rather quickly, to the address that was on the index card. Which happened to be Lindsey's old house on Alyssa street in Lakewood.

LAKEWOOD HAD QUIETED down now that the asshole that was causing the problems had been dealt with two years ago and people had started to move back in. For some reason though Lindsey's house was still unoccupied. He wasn't sure why, but for now he was thankful. Because after everything he had experienced in Lakewood he knew that a random card with the address of his deceased lover showing up in the mail was not really random at all. There was a reason and he was going to find out what it was.

He pulled into the driveway and quickly made his way to the front door and that was when he saw another index card taped to the door. He pulled the index card off and saw that his name was printed on the front, just like the last, but on the back was just one word: Kitchen.

Even more confused he reached down and turned the door knob and was surprised to see that it was not locked and that it swung open with ease. He practically lived in this house for a while before moving into Jerry's old house on Veronica street, so he knew the layout really well and wasted no time going to the kitchen.

He paused in the empty front room and sighed. All of her furniture was gone. Which he shouldn't be surprised about. Still he was on a mission and had no time to wallow in self pity so he hurried into the kitchen and was once more greeted by an index card that was taped to the front of the fridge.

Like the first two this one had his name on it as well and on the other side there were two words: Bedroom Closet.

He turned the card over in his hand smiling. This was definitely something Lindsey would do. She always tried to do little clever scavenger hunts for him. Hunts that just led them to bed where they wound up making love. Of course her being a spirit meant that sex was not going to happen, that did not change the fact though that he would indeed like what he found at the end of this little mystery.

With no hesitation he bounded up the stairs two at a time and before he knew it he was walking in the bedroom where some of his best memories were to be had. He looked at the spot where Lindsey's bed once sat and smiled. He honestly was happy with Lindsey for a full year before she was taken from him. And he knew he would achieve that happiness again. But for now he needed to mourn and understand his loss.

He walked over to the closet and opened it and was surprised when he saw the small shoebox on the shelf. He pulled it down and found himself carrying it into the center of the room. He then sat down and put the shoebox in his lap before opening it. The first thing he noticed was a picture of him and Lindsey. One of the few they took together. Underneath the photo were stacks of notes and pages of writing all in Lindsey's handwriting. He pulled out the first note and realized that it was indeed to him.

He read the note and even though it was just four lines he could help but shed a tear. The note simply said that she truly loved him and in the box were her memories of their time together and their adventures through what happened in Lakewood. He laughed out loud when he read the headline of one of the notes which simply read:

Scary Things Happen in Lakewood.

He could not help but to laugh. Lindsey had documented everything that had happened. Not to mention found time to tell him how much she loved him. Even from the great beyond she had managed to somehow pull off one last scavenger hunt. Albeit a simple one. He was pretty sure there was only so much a spirit could do. Standing up with a smile and tears on his face Cliff made sure to carefully place the lid back on the box. He then tucked it under his arm and stood in the empty room for a moment.

"I love you too baby," He said out loud. Then he turned and left.

He walked out of the house and towards the car. Gently setting the box down in the passenger seat and just before he pulled out of the familiar driveway. He looked at the house and made a promise.

"I'll let the world know," He promised as he patted the lid to the box. "I will let them all know." Then he pulled out of the driveway and down Alyssa street. Never once looking back. He had just gotten his closure and his future was now directly ahead of him. He was now ready for whatever life had in store for him.

THE END

The Devil Drives A GTO

Trevor knew what he was doing was wrong, yet it was easy money. All he had to do was drive the van. The man he was introduced to, who called himself Hammer sat in the passenger seat, holding a sawed off shotgun. The third guy, a more normal name of Carl, sat in the back on a milkcrate armed with a forty five. He was keeping an eye on their cargo. Four women whose only crime was being in the wrong place at the wrong time.

Trevor had years of experience as a wheelman. He couldn't remember doing anything else with his life. His first and only legit job was delivering pizzas, which is how he got his start of learning the ins and outs of maneuvering a vehicle at high speeds.

A cousin of Trevors needed a wheelman for a simple bank robbery and the one wheelman they had lined up was pinched for trying to boost cars. So he asked Trevor if he could help. All Trevor needed to do was drive. It was a simple smash and grab. That was it.

Trevor's skills were immediately noticed. Trevor himself couldn't quite explain how he was able to maneuver the car the way he did. It was like instinct. Trevor was just a natural driver and the entire underworld took notice.

Soon Trevor was driving more and more. His paydays after each gig, growing. Soon he only needed to drive four to five times a year. Because Trevor managed his money wisely and he never got caught. Hell the police didn't even have a clue on who was driving. Which is something every wheelman wants. Soon he was being considered for more high profile crimes. Which led him to being behind the wheel of the van he was driving .

Trevor never felt a twinge of guilt during any of his crimes. Because it was just money. Sometimes he drove cargo across the country. But never live people. Being involved in a human trafficking ring was something different and something that did weigh heavy on his conscience.For the first time in his career as a driver Trevor felt guilt. And something else.

Fear.

He wasn't afraid of getting caught. It was Hammer that really bothered him. The guy just did not seem stable. Twice he had threatened to go back there and sample the "merchandise". With Carl explaining that the women are not to be touched until the Prince gets to have them first. Hammer did not like it and had threatened to kill them all. Cleary the guy was a lunatic and a rapist.

Trevor just kept thinking about the payday. Because that was the only thing that was keeping him from turning tail and running. The curator of this job had said that the client was a wealthy prince from the Middle East, who paid a lot of money for four young, American, white girls. If they pulled it off and delivered their cargo to the docks by midnight they each would receive just over two million dollars.

That was why Trevor was doing this. That kind of money meant that he could take plenty of time off. Travel, enjoy what was left of his twenties. Maybe find a different calling in life. Two million dollars bought you a life if you knew how to spend it correctly.

So here he was on a dark stretch of road. The only car for miles heading towards a dock that was rarely used. All he had to do was get the van there by midnight and he was an hour ahead of schedule.

"Hey Carl" Hammer spoke up, "Look the prince won't know if I took a round with the pretty little redhead. She's practically begging for it, Being tied up is making that bitch hot I can smell it." Hammer then took a deep breath through his nose to signal that he was indeed picking up her scent.

"Goddamn man," Carl retorted, "No fucking names, and no you will not touch any of these women."

"Ptth" Hammer protested, "Who the fuck are they gonna tell, they gonna be used and abused, locked in a palace until they like it. Second how the fuck will he know I took me a turn."

"Because he plans on using them the minute they are on his yacht." Carl answered. "And if he sees that they were touched in any way we are all dead."

"Fuck, whatever" Hammer said before sitting back in his seat.

Trevor could hear the girls cry and strain against their restraints after hearing Carl reveal their fate. But he did not turn around; he just stared ahead. Keeping his eyes on the road. Checking the side mirrors every few minutes to see if they were being followed. The road was normally empty this time of year due to the migration patterns of deer making it hard to travel. Which is why Trevor requested an extra large bull bar to be installed on the front of the van. He knew this road would be empty and if he was lucky he would not have to go over fifty miles and hour. Easy trip, easy drive, easy money.

The road behind them had been empty for a while now, so Trevor was surprised to see the reflection of head lights in the distance about a good mile or so away.

"Hmm" Trevor said out loud.

"What's hmm?" Carl asked.

"A set of headlights, in the mirror" Trevor answered. "Coming fast too. Could be some hot rodder racing down this road, adrenaline junkie looking for a fix."

"Is it a problem?" Hammer asked.

"Don't know?" Trevor answered. "If it's what I think it is, he will just blow right past us, and we may see him upside down a few miles down the road."

"Just keep an eye on it," Carl ordered.

"Yep," Trevor replied.

So with one eye on the road and another on the driver side mirror Trevor kept the van pushing forward as the headlights came closer and closer. Soon the car was close enough that Trevor was able to identify it.

It was a Pontiac GTO. A 1970 model if Trevor wasn't mistaken. The headlight placement left little doubt that it was indeed a vintage model. Why someone would be racing a classic muscle car down a dangerous stretch of road at night was a mystery to him. Yet here he was transporting four women to a fate worse than death. So someone else's questionable actions weren't really for him to question.

Before he knew it the GTO was just a car length behind them. Slowing to match their speed. Then as it began to keep a pace with the van the driver began to honk the horn.

"Holy shit is that what I think it is?" Carl asked.

Trevor did not answer. Instead he pressed the accelerator of the van and began to speed forward. Yet as he sped up so did the GTO.

"Cops?" Carl asked.

"No!" Trevor answered. "There are no cherries on the roof, I think it is just some asshole pissed he had to slow down. Give him a minute and he may just pass us."

Instead of passing the GTO's horn blared loudly once more.

"Oh fuck this guy," Hammer said, as he rolled down the window and began to lean out, pointing his gun in the direction of the GTO.

Before anyone could stop him, Hammer managed to squeeze off three shots. Trevor watched in the mirror as sparks ricocheted off the hood of the car as each bullet hit its target.

What happened next shocked everyone.

Trevor knew that the damage probably caused by Hammer's handgun was purely surface damage if anything. Yet the entire GTO slowly burst into flames. Not like a slow flame either. It was like a match head. Just a whoosh and they were now being chased by GTO shaped fireball.

Hammer was still hanging out the window watching as the car burst into flames. Trevor could hear the asshole cheering, as if his bullets had done what they all just witnessed. Yet even Carl knew something wasn't right, having watched the car burst into flames from the rear window of the van.

"Man get your stupid ass into this car, something is not right," Carl demanded. 'Before adding "holy hell did it just get hot in here."

Hammer must have heard him because his cheering abruptly stopped, and from the corner of his eye Trevor could see Hammer sliding back into the window, yet what he saw wasn't right, because the only thing sliding back down into the passenger seat was Hammer's lower half. His entire upper half was gone.

There was no blood, Hammer's waist where his top half should have been was smoldering, it was like it was cauterized. Something extremely hot and powerful had just obliterated half of Hammer.

"What the fuck!" Carl shouted.

Trevor had an idea that whatever was happening with the GTO was not natural. The half of Hammer's charred corpse was proof. So he ignored Carl's shouting and instead pressed his foot down on the gas pedal, racing the van forward. While Carl began to lose his mind, Trevor, like any good wheelman, stayed focused on the road ahead. Because driving this fast was something that required all of his attention and he could not afford any lapse in concentration.

"Where the fuck is the rest of Hammer?" Carl Shouted, "What the fuck is going on?"

Trevor ignored him and pushed the gas pedal down even further, pushing the aging van as fast as it could possibly go. Trevor was so focused on the road ahead he barely noticed when Carl opened the back doors.

Thankfully the four women were blindfolded because they were spared the sight of what happened next.

Carl effortlessly kicked the doors on the back of the van open and brought his forty-five up and quickly began to fire off shot after shot. Each bullet bounced harmlessly off the flaming GTO. Once the firearm was empty Carl ejected the clip and went to reload. Unfortunately for him a large tendril made of swirling flame erupted from the hood of the GTO. It moved with an insane quickness, and slammed into Carl's chest. Just as soon as the tendril made contact, Carl just exploded.

Trevor heard the pop, he was too focused on the road ahead to see what had happened, but he felt some of Carl's blood splatter onto the back of his head. The women in the back were showered with blood and whatever parts of Carl that were not immediately liquified. Turning the entire rear of the van into a cave of crimson soaked gore.

Trevor knew he had to escape whatever was chasing him. He didn't care if he made it to the docks or onto a crowded highway, hell even into the parking lot of a police station. Just as long as it got him away from whatever was driving that demonic GTO. Every fiber of his being was telling him to look in the rearview mirror, to look at the flaming vehicle that was chasing him down. Trevor ignored those thoughts and stared straight ahead. So when the black deer that seemed to rise out of the shadows suddenly appeared in front of him he was indeed taken by surprise.

Slamming both feet on the brake pedal Trevor struggled to keep the van under his control. It began to fishtail as the wheels skid across the dusty asphalt. The girls were thrown forward on top of each other as the brakes locked and the van began to slow to a stop. The black deer was growing closer and closer as Trevor braced for impact. He closed his eyes and waited, and was surprised when the van came to a stop. He opened his eyes and saw that the deer was no longer there. The violent braking had somehow caused the engine to stall, so Trevor slammed the van back into park and began to turn the ignition hoping to start the engine. He finally looked into the rear view and saw that the vans doors were still open and that the GTO, now no longer on fire, was parked directly behind him. Trevor shook his head and tried turning the engine over once more when the driver side window suddenly imploded.

Trevor felt two strong hands grab him by the collar of his shirt and before he could react he found himself being pulled awkwardly through the broken window. It was fast and with such force that he was pretty sure his right leg was broken as he was violently pulled free from the van. He had little time to think about what was happening before he was thrown hard onto his back onto the road, and everything suddenly started to hurt. He was able to look up at his assailant and he saw a well dressed man in a dark red suit, with black tie and what looked to be gator skin shoes standing over him.

"My God kid you are good," The man said cheerfully, "But you ain't that good."

"Who are you,?" Trevor asked breathlessly.

"Geuss." The man responded with a laugh, "Here let me give you a hint." The man paused then sang out, "Please allow me to introduce myself. I'm a man of wealth and taste." Then he spread out his arms as if what he just did gave away the obvious answer.

"What?" Trevor asked, not understanding the "ta-da" moment.

"Seriously?" The man responded, "Does no one listen to the stones anymore," He threw his arms up disgustedly, "Oh well it doesn't really matter." He then turned around and shouted towards the van. "Hey ladies you're safe and a little birdie tipped off the cops and they are on they're way to save you." He then turned and walked over to Trevor where he stood over his head and looked down into Trevor's eyes.

Trevor looked up and with tears flowing down his cheek pleaded, "Please no."

"Now now don't you cry," The man retorted with a laugh, "It will be quick and when I am done with you I am going to the docks where I get to murder me a prince and sink a fucking million dollar yacht, now that my dear boy is a good damn productive night."

The man stood up and raised his right foot over Trevor's head preparing to stomp down onto the wheelman's skull.

Just before the GTO driver's foot came down, smashing his skull to paste, and killing him, Trevor finally realized who the man really was.

THE END

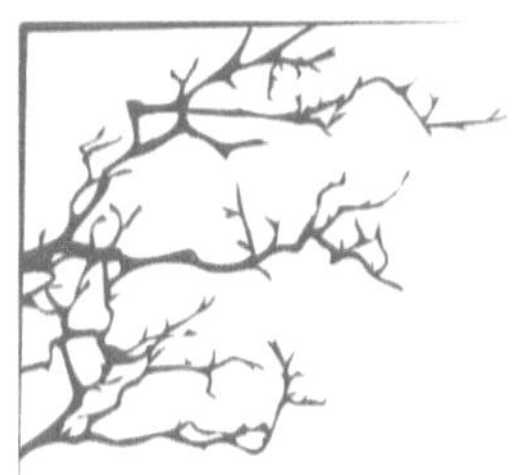

Catch

Liam's father demanded perfection. But only in the thing that mattered to him, which happened to be baseball. Liam's father was a drunkard, a wife beater, and an alpha male, complete with toxic mentality and all. He was also a failed baseball player who was kicked out of the minor leagues. Now a carpet salesman, Liam's father was going to live his dream through Liam. Liam though did not like baseball, which caused him to feel his father's wrath more than once. Especially when his father would force Liam outside to play catch. Which led to Liam suffering some form of physical or emotional humiliation. Over every dropped ball or poorly executed throw.

The neighbors of course knew what kind of man Liam's father was. How could they not. Liam's father would unleash a slew of harsh criticisms and abuse towards his son outside. Of course they constantly checked on Liam and his mother whenever his father would leave. They would offer condolences, and food. Claim that they would help them if they chose to escape. Yet they were never there to confront Liam's father. The neighbor's would always offer support from the safety of their own homes. Sometimes watching the abuse play out.

Well almost all of them There was one neighbor who did not hide her disdain for Liam's father. Her name was Rosalie.

Rosalie was a different kind of woman. She was single, and lived alone with what appeared to be a small army of cats. Liam would find himself passing her house each day he walked to school and he would always notice a different cat in her windows. Sure sometimes the same cat would reappear. Or maybe Liam's mind could not keep up with the sheer number of cats this woman might have. Whatever the case whenever he passed her house he felt an overwhelming sense of safety when he did. The cats never appeared to be aggressive or men as they watched him. It was as if they were concerned, perhaps even protective of him.

Sometimes Rosalie would be on her porch in the afternoon when he passed by. She would offer a friendly wave and even encourage him to keep his head up. Liam of course would not return the wave. He would lower his head from her gaze and hurry home. Because Liam's father had repeatedly warned him that Rosalie was a witch and that she was an agent of Satan and that she hurt children.

Liam was not completely sure if his father was telling the truth. Matter of fact the warnings about Rosalie did not start until right after Rosalie confronted his father. In public.

In the small town in which he lived there was only one grocery store. It was a well stocked grocer with fair prices. It went by the name of Brady's. Liam loved going to Brady's because out front near the registers was a small room with four video game cabinets. It was outside that room where people saw the monster his dad could be. It was also there that Rosalie confronted his father.

Like most children Liam could lose track of time while playing video games. Normally it wasn't a problem. His mother would check in before ringing up the groceries and tell him to hurry up, and he would. The only time it became an issue was when Liam's father decided to go shopping with them. He would humiliate Liam for having any other interests besides baseball. Video games were a distraction. A waste of time. Liam enjoyed the bright spectacle and how they would just light a whole room. He even began to show an interest in how they were made and wanted to study and perhaps learn how video games were made, just so he could possibly create his own one day.

One particular Saturday Liam's family decided to go shopping as a group. Well not so much decided as his father demanded that he go, because it was to be a nice day and Liam needed to play catch for as long as the sun was up. So by going Liam's father ensured that the shopping trip would be quick.

The shopping outing was indeed hurried. Liam's father would grab select items that he felt they needed and not what was actually on the grocery list. It was awkward to say the least. So Liam snuck off and made his way to the small arcade. He had a good handful of quarters and began to play his favorite cabinet. The room was usually unoccupied this early on a Saturday and Liam wanted to have some enjoyment before his father ruined his weekend with his forced game of catch.

Soon his parents were checking out and in the quickness of it all Liam's mother forgot to tell them they were checking out. Leaving Liam in the middle of a game when his father walked into the arcade and told Liam it was time to go.

"Just a minute dad," Liam responded. He did not think it would be a problem, until his father grabbed him by the back of his neck and jerked him away from the arcade cabinet. Hoping to prove a point LIam's father did not let go and instead began to drag him out of the small arcade and into the front of the store. Calling Liam a colorful collection of names one should never call a child.

The entire front of the store let out a collective gasp. While offended no one stepped up to call out his father or attempt to tell him to stop. Well that was until Rosalie walked in.

The automatic doors slid open and Rosalie stood there effectively blocking his father's path. She stood there with her arms folded across her chest and in a stern loud voice said, "You need to let your son go now."

Another gasp sounded out from the people who were now gathering at the registers. Liam's father though was unbothered. "Shut up bitch," He replied, "and get the fuck out of my way."

Liam had heard his father swear before, just never in public. He could feel his father's grip loosen on his neck though which he found odd. Undaunted Rosalie stood in his way and reiterated her demand. "Let your son go now."

To his surprise Liam felt his father let him go and once he found his feet he ran past Rosalie and towards his mom who was watching everything from just outside the door.

Liam turned and heard Rosalie say, "You ever hurt your son or wife again, there will be hell to pay."

Liam's father scoffed and pushed his way past Rosalie who stepped aside just enough for him to pass. He pointed at Liam's mom and yelled, "Get the shit in the car" before storming past. He then got into the car and started the engine. The entire time staring angrily over the steering wheel.

It took Liam and his mother seconds to load the car before long they too climbed inside it. His father practically broke the sound barrier as he sped out of the parking lot and headed home.

The entire ride home was uncomfortable to say the least. Liam's father called Rosalie every name in the book and then some. Neither he nor his mother responded to his father's ramblings and anger induced diatribe. Instead they allowed his father the time to vent and get it out of his system. By the time they had arrived home Liam's father had begun to calm down slightly. Which was a relief because Liam knew that as soon as he helped his mother with the groceries his father's twisted game of catch would begin.

The carrying in of groceries took little to no time at all and before Liam could even take a breath his father was calling for him to get outside. Because baseball was indeed his father's life and Liam was going to learn to like it.

Now if it was to be just an innocent game of catch as most kids did with their father Liam wouldn't become overwhelmed with anxiety whenever his father suggested they play catch. His father was a bully behind closed doors, but the abuse he would inflict after a bad game of catch was indeed horrific. A Lot of times his father would just call him names and embarrass him. Sometimes though his father would turn the baseball they were practicing with into a projectile weapon and throw it at Liam with such velocity that if it contacted any part of Liam's body he would be bruised and sore for weeks.

Liam reluctantly grabbed his ball cap and glove and headed outside where his father was already waiting for him. His father was casually staring in the direction of Rosalie's house muttering something to himself. The expression on his face was a mixture of annoyance and anger. That caused Liam's heart to drop because he knew right away that this game of catch was definitely going to start off abusive.

"Take your position boy," Liam's father growled.

Liam had heard that tone before and practically winced when he heard it. Liam slowly made his way to the other side of the yard and turned around. He barely had his glove at the ready when his dad threw a line drive fast ball towards him. Liam moved and caught the ball in his glove yet even with the thick leather glove on the ball stung his hand. Liam hissed with his teeth and let out an "Ow,"

"Are you fucking kidding me boy," His father shouted from across the yard, "First throw and you're gonna puss out?"

"No sir!" Liam answered. He then took the ball out of his glove and threw it back to his father. The throw was fairly decent and it sailed across the yard and directly into his father's glove.

"Nice throw son," His father said, "but you can do better." Then without hesitation threw another near violent pitch at Liam.

Even though Liam had his glove up the ball was a little two high and fast for Liam's eyes to see and before he could react the ball flew over his glove and slammed off his upper bicep. The pain was instantaneous and to Liam it felt as if his entire arm had just gone numb. He did the only thing an eleven year old knew how to do when this kind of pain is inflicted upon them. He screamed out and began to cry. Reaching up with his free arm to rub the area that the baseball had just struck.

"Jesus Christ!" His father shouted out. "Shut up and grab the ball, quit being a little bitch."

With tears still in his eyes Liam walked over and grabbed the ball he then threw it back to his father. The throw was a bit high and Liam's father had to jump in the air slightly to catch it.

"What the fuck was that?" His father screamed. "I should never have to go out of my way to catch a ball." Then before Liam knew what was happening his father had thrown another fastball in his direction.

Liam's mother had heard the commotion outside and stepped onto the porch just in time to see her husband throw a wicked fastball at their son. Liam was not able to move this time and the ball struck the young boy in the stomach. Knowing she needed to intervene she bolted off the porch and towards her son. Yelling at her husband as she went.

"What the hell is wrong with you?" She shouted as she ran past her husband.

"Oh come on now he's not hurt." Liam's father responded. "Besides he's gonna get hit with a lot more baseballs out on the field, he needs to get used to it."

Liam's mother paused for a moment to reach down and pick up the baseball and she turned and hurled it in the direction of her husband, who plucked it out of the air with ease. "Well maybe baseball just isn't his thing," She retorted before she turned and approached Liam who was still doubled over on the ground holding his stomach and crying. "Baby you ok," she asked.

The crack sound the ball made when it slammed into her back was practically deafening and everything just sorta of slowed down for Liam. The pain in his stomach subsided a bit as his mother fell to her knees screaming. Even over her screams of pain he could hear every word his father said.

"Listen here you stupid bitch," He shouted, "My son will indeed be a ball player. You don't have a clue how much better his life will be once he is. Just take your ass inside and leave us alone." He then paused and added, "Now Liam get the fuck up and.."

Something strange happened before his father could finish his sentence. Liam's father just stopped talking. There was a brief silence followed by a loud piercing scream as Liam's father's legs suddenly burst into flames.

At first that was what it looked like to Liam. His father had just started to spontaneously combust. But once he was able to blink the tears and pain from his eyes everything came into focus. Liam's father's legs hadn't just caught on fire. The ground had suddenly opened up underneath his father and columns of flame were erupting out from underneath him. Liam's mother turned around and she too was stunned into silence as the flames began to grow higher and higher.

Within seconds Liam's father was completely engulfed in flames. The man's screaming had stopped and instead all they could hear was the roar of the fire. Then what looked to be hands made of total darkness erupted out of the ground and Liam's father was quickly pulled into the ground. There was a brief flash of light and then nothing except a small smoldering spot on the ground where Liam's father had just stood.

Liam and his mother stood up and just started at the smoking patch of earth where his father had once been. They nearly jumped out of their skin when they heard a voice speak up beside them.

"I did warn him" The voice said.

Liam and his mother turned and saw that Rosalie was now standing next to them. In her arms was a fat orange tom cat who looked to be asleep. Rosalie smiled at them and slowly walked over to the small patch of earth that was now regaining its color as the smoke began to subside.

"That's that," Rosalie said, she then turned and faced Liam and his mother and in a friendly warm tone of voice spoke, "Don't cry for him, because you are both safe now."

Liam smiled because, well he did not feel like crying.

THE END

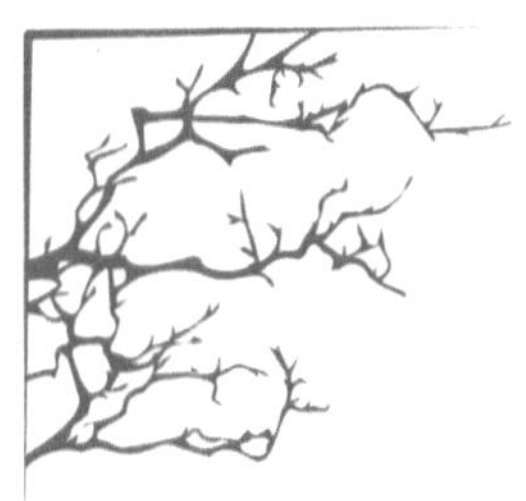

I Tried

I tried to be a better man
   I tried to keep my hands clean
I tried to have a brighter future
I tried to keep my hands clean
I tried to live a good life
I tried to shine bright like the sun
I tried to be a good example
I tried to be someone
I tried to do my best
I tried to not fail
I tried to sit on top of the world
I tried to stay out of Hell
I tried

I FAILED.
   I am sorry that I let you down
   I failed
   And now I'll no longer be around

I AM SORRY.

05-03-1988

...TEENAGE ANGST AM I right. This was written during my last year of high school. I must have been depressed. But I made it through. Hey, not everything has an explanation. Maybe someone feeling down needs to know other people feel that same feeling as well. You're loved whoever you are....

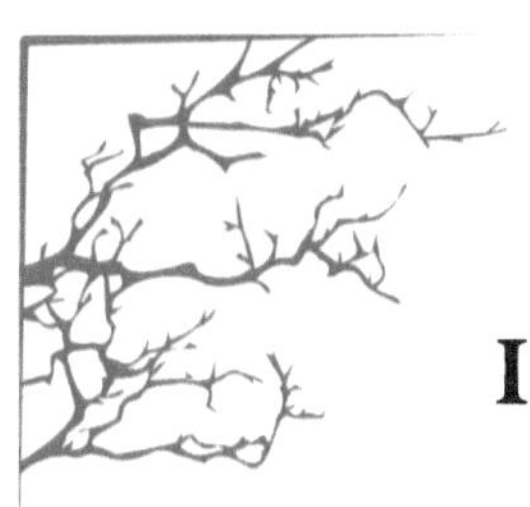

I F@&king Hate Christmas

*T*rigger Warning...The following story contains a scene and plot centered around a mass shooting. As an author who writes horror I tend to write about things that bother or frighten me. Feel free to skip this story. I will understand. Also I wouldn't know if you did. It's ok to not want to read something that makes you uncomfortable. If you continue please remember you were warned.*

I DIDN'T ALWAYS HATE Christmas. In fact I loved it. The festive lights, the music, the magic. I literally ate that shit up. I do not remember my first Christmas. I do, though, recall several good ones.I even have pleasant photos that I can look at to celebrate those memories. If I concentrate I can even taste the food my grandmother would make. From her coconut cake to her ham. I remember every great gift. Every laugh that was shared around the Christmas tree. Yet all of those memories are constantly overshadowed by the memory of when I began to really hate the holidays.

I WAS ELEVEN YEARS old and I had started to suspect Santa Claus wasn't real. I mean the idea of a Mall Santa in every single mall across the nation was my first real indication that something was amiss. I had even started an investigation with my cousin who lived in Minneapolis. We would beg our mother to take us to see our Santa on the same day. It was childish yet in our minds we knew that it would prove inconclusively that Santa wasn't real. Because after all no matter how strong Christmas magic actually was there was no way Santa could be in two malls at the same time giving out candy canes. Quick air travel by reindeer was one thing, instantaneous travel, well that was just unheard of.

That was how our little innocent eleven year old brains worked. We hatched a scheme to prove something. To us it was complicated. To our mothers it was just them living up to an annual tradition. Of course cell phones were not a thing back in the eighties, but we had landlines.So the plan was after we sat on our laps, got our candy canes, and arrived home, we were going to call each other and compare notes. It was a simple plan. Not worthy of a Christmas special of course, yet a holiday adventure nevertheless.

Me and my cousin had convinced our mothers to take us to see Santa at friday. While we were two states away we were still in the same time zone. So we managed to get our mothers to take us to see the mall Santa in our town at the same time. We were going to get that evidence we so desired.

While my cousin had a pleasant and memorable outing at the mall with his mother. My evening was a night of total terror.

The evening started out innocently enough. My father stayed at home to catch up on paperwork from his job. So it was just a mother, son date night. We started the evening by going to a local fast food burger joint. I got a kids meal that in retrospect I was too old for, and an ice cream cone. Then we went to our local mall. Which already had a full parking lot. Yet my mom,being who she was, managed to get a spot close to the west entrance. It was just luck that she pulled up just as someone was leaving. We arrived at the mall at six when we walked inside we saw that the line to see Santa was already quite long. There were close to a hundred children all chatting, crying, or laughing as they prepared to see good ole Kris Kringle.

The line itself never spilled outside. The center court of the mall was large enough for them to create a zigzag queue line so we were all able to stand inside. Yet with all the children making noise at once the center court was extremely loud as a multitude of voices echoed throughout the entire area.

I of course made my own fair share of noise as I occasionally shouted out in excitement, or a greeting to someone I knew from school. The joyful sound of children laughing was high in the air. A true sign that the holiday season was upon us. Of course what happened just precious minutes later turned the entire holiday season into a nightmare for those that survived.

Now no one knows why he did it. Not even to this day. He was apparently a nice neighbor, a wonderful husband and father, a hardworking employee. He volunteered to be a mall Santa just so he could spread cheer. Well according to those that were close to him. I never knew the guy so my perspective on the situation was that he was a monster and he waited for the exact moment to unleash hell onto as many people as possible.

The throne Santa sat on was on a three foot high platform that allowed him to look out at the sea of smiling children, and afforded every child the chance to look up at him. It was truly a magical experience. So when he walked out on that platform from behind the oversized backdrop and throne every child immediately noticed the bright red suit, the white beard, the large bell, and each child fully believed that good ole Saint Nick was here.

Not a single one of us noticed the gun that hung by its strap loosely at his side.

As a matter of fact only a couple of the adults that were in line with their children noticed the gun. The rest of them were looking down at their excited happy kids. Some of them for the last time. Because the Santa on the platform wasted no time. As soon as he was at the edge of the platform he brought the gun up from his side and with no hesitation or warning he opened fire. He managed to squeeze off three rounds before people started to react.

My mother went to attention almost immediately. She grabbed my hand and tried to pull me away. Yet I was practically frozen in place. I watched as the world around me slowed down as the Psycho Santa (as the press would eventually call him) shot downward into the crowd of excited children.

It wasn't quite like fish in a barrel, but close enough.

At the angle and distance Psycho Santa had, he did not need to be good at aiming.Nope almost every bullet he fired hit a target. Most of them were fatal shots. Soon the joyous laughter and excited cheers from children turned to loud screaming and panicked cries as bodies and blood began to coat the center court floor of the mall. And like an idiot I just stood there.

My mother was screaming and pulling my hand when the crowd surged and tried to turn and run. Yet the ridiculous queue line created by mall staff prevented them from really moving. As some managed to trip and knock over the barriers that were set up others took advantage and began to trample the ones that had fallen. The fathers who had survived the initial gunfire were now scooping up their children, some dead, some alive. And were leading the charge. Meanwhile the Psycho Santa on the platform reloaded his gun and was heading down the stairs that the children would take when greeting him. Once he was on the floor he raised his rifle and once more opened fire on the crowd that was now attempting to run away from him.

Somehow my mother found the strength to lift my eleven year old slightly chubby frame off the ground. Then as she carried me in both arms close to her chest she took off running towards the exit of the mall. Which wasn't that far seeing as we were close to the back of the line, and the people behind us had long since left and were already exiting the mall.

The way she carried me I was still able to see the Psycho Santa as he continued to open fire on the fleeing crowd. I watch adults fall and crash to the ground, some landing on top of their children. Others managed to fall to their knees, pushing their children away from them and with their last breaths telling their kids to run. Through the entire ordeal I don't remember being scared. The feeling I felt was weird. I was never able to quite explain. Well not until now.

The only time I felt any real form of terror was when my mother suddenly cried out. Just like that the world sped back up and I realized that we were falling to the ground. My mother fell to her knees and I found myself holding her up as my feet hit the ground. I looked into my mothers face and saw blood flowing from the corners of her mouth. She let one hand slip from my shoulder and down to her stomach and that was when I noticed the nice sized wound in her abdomen. Psycho Santa had shot my mom and the bullet managed to miss me. Somehow.

Tears filled my eyes as I looked into her face. I could see the pain on hers, yet that didn't stop her from pushing me away with her free hand as she yelled at me to run. Then she fell over to her side. I did not run. I immediately knelt beside my mother and began to call out to her. Then I heard men start to scream out, "Freeze" and "Drop your weapon" before more gunshots rang out.

I looked up and saw that Psycho Santa was now having a gunfight with the police who had just arrived. Good ole Saint Nick never stood a chance. A barrage of bullets shredded the man and he was soon falling to the ground. His bright festive red Santa suit now stained crimson. I watched the horrific scene play out before me, and I did not turn away until I felt a strong hand grab me by the shoulders and pulled me to my feet. The last thing I did in the mall that day was look down at my mother and the growing pool of blood that started to surround her.

Thirty people died that day. Seventeen children, ten parents, two police officers and the Psycho Santa. And just like that our town was on the map. There was a media storm that followed, with reporters parked in front of the house of nearly every survivor. For weeks it was front page news. My father took me to my grandmother's house to escape it. Yet the reporters managed to follow us there as well. The media dubbed him the Psycho Santa at first. Until they knew his name and then the guy was famous. Everyone knew his name. Yet no one knew the name of any of the survivors. None of the victims. Yet the maniac who just gunned down thirty people went from a quiet respectable neighbor, to a celebrity.

That really shocked me.

The trauma of the entire thing affected me a little differently than most. Sure I missed my mom and I began to loathe the holidays. Yet I could not get over just how famous Psycho Santa had become. As the years passed stories about the horrible events at my mall grew in scale. There were even two movies made about it. One a television event that warned about the dangers of such men. And the other was a major motion picture that actually told a sympathetic story from the killer's point of view. The film even won two oscars. I just could not believe it. I watched my schoolmates and my mother die.Yet all anyone could remember was Santa with a Gun.

YEARS AND YEARS PASSED. I went to therapy, I buried my father, and just sorta went on with my life. I got a decent job. Found a girl and lived a happy life. Yet I always felt empty inside. I wasn't sure what I was missing. Until I found myself applying to be a mall Santa.

Surprisingly getting the job as a Santa required more of a background check then getting a semi automatic rifle.

I knew what I wanted. I have wanted it ever since that day in the mall. I wanted fame. I wanted notoriety. I wanted to be remembered. I knew living a boring average life was going to get me nowhere. But this. Oh yeah this is going to make me famous.

And that's really it. That's why I bought this gun. That is why I am dressed in this silly looking fatsuit. I have grown to really hate the holidays. Yet in retrospect it is what made me the man I am today. My gun is loaded. I am dressed for my big moment and soon I will go out there and just make a name for myself. Just like the last guy who did this.

Pay it forward, I guess.

Some of you may be disgusted by what I am about to do and that is fine. But you will know me. Some of you will be sympathetic to my story. My past. But you will all know my name. My legend will grow and soon you will be watching a movie made about me. Because after all that's what we do. We become addicted to the things we hate. Like a vampire to blood we turn on the news hoping to hear about some kind of tragedy so we can talk about it the next day. I didn't really want to do this. I needed to. Because we all want to be remembered. And who knows maybe I will inspire the next Psycho Santa or whatever clever nickname the media gives me. Whatever the case, you already know me.

And you will never forget me.

THE END

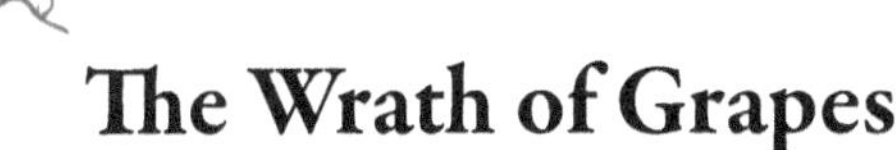

The Wrath of Grapes

When Eric moved out to California with his wife Sharon and purchased their own vineyard they had high hopes and dreams of owning their own prosperous wine company. Unfortunately they discovered that starting a successful wine business was going to take a lot more than just hopes and dreams.

Growing grapes did not turn out to be as simple as they believed. Then came the process of making the wine. They quickly learned just how difficult this venture was going to be.

He had purchased the old vineyard for next to nothing. The agent who sold him the property mentioned something about the place having a bad history. Rumors of mysterious deaths. Which was why no one had purchased the property. Eric could not believe it. There were rows upon rows of trellis, some with grapes still growing on them. Why no one showed an interest in this property for the past thirty years was insane. Even with the rumors and negative history surrounding the place.

Sharon of course looked up information about the property. Apparently the vineyard was built on sacred ground that once belonged to the ancient tribe of indigenous people who once called themselves the Serrano tribe. Of course their land was taken over and a vineyard was erected. Only two families had ever owned the vineyard. The first moved after several of their workers and servants began to vanish. Or worse suffer a horrific death. The second family purchased it for cheap and just vanished off the face of the Earth. After that urban legends surrounding the vineyard began to grow. There were even stories, mostly passed around by the locals, about people that would disappear near the vineyard. It had even become a dare among the teenagers, seeing if any of them were brave enough to walk through the vineyard after dark. Of course the more the legends and rumors grew the less people believed them. That still did not make Sharon comfortable about purchasing the place.

Eric was a dreamer and God help her she loved him. He had inherited a good sum of money when his mother passed. They could have stayed in Iowa and lived a good life. Unfortunately Eric wanted to make a name for himself and that was when he discovered the vineyard and suddenly he knew he just needed to become a winemaker. It was indeed his claim to fame. The same thing he said about being a comedian, a youtube sensation and the world's best car salesmen. She did not believe the winemaking would take off, but the land and beautiful house was worth the expenditure and the move. She always fancied herself a California girl and now thanks to her husband's wild fantasy she was going to get to live it. There was no way they would run out of money. Sure they would need jobs eventually, but right now she figured she might as well enjoy it. She also had just enough of a positive attitude that she believed that maybe, just maybe, Eric might find success.

Unfortunately he had no idea what he was doing.

Within two weeks of moving in and with Eric touring and tending to the grapes using online online video tutorials as a guide, the vines began to wither and go brown. The grapes he did manage to harvest rotted before he even had a chance to process them. So he wasn't even able to figure out how to properly make wine. Not willing to give up, Eric went into town to find help, and supplies. Because he did not want to let go of his dream just yet.

At a local hardware store Eric bumped into a man by the name of Luis. Luis asked him who he was and what he was looking for. After a brief conversation Luis agreed to check out Eric's grapevines and offer some sound advice and assistance. For a fee of course. A fee that Eric was willing to pay. Because his life was now all about the vineyard. He did not want to fail.

Sharon was a little surprised that Eric went out and hired someone to help. But she was not going to complain. Because it looked as if Eric was indeed taking his attempted venture into winemaking seriously. When the man he had hired, a pleasant fellow by the name of Luis, showed up to investigate the vineyard she was thrilled. That day Eric and Luis toured the trellis and the gardens. While she stayed behind and made a full meal for both the men. When they returned she eavesdropped on their conversation and was happy to hear Luis tell her husband how the plants were indeed healthy. How the soil was rich and full of life. Luis continued by saying that he could easily bring every grape plant back to life, all he needed was one day with a small crew of workers. There was some brush and overgrowth to be clear, and the plants themselves could use a little attention. Other than that the grapes would be back to full health and Eric would soon be able to start making his own wine. The price Luis listed for doing the work was indeed fair and affordable, so Eric and Sharon both agreed to allow Luis and his small team the chance to fix the grapevines.

That night after Luis left they made love for the first time since arriving in California.

The following morning Luis and a team of four men arrived bright and early. Eric walked with them to the vineyard. Each man carried a collection of tools while one pushed a wheelbarrow loaded with spades and hoes. Eric asked if he needed to stay and help, he was quickly dismissed by Luis who told him that Eric paid for his work and that he could just go back to his house and relax. Which was indeed what Eric did.

Hours passed and soon the sun was high in the air. Sharon and Eric both began to wonder what Luis and his team were up to. You could not really see them or the vineyards from the house thanks to a few large trees that grew around the property so before she set to making lunch Sharon decided to go down into the vineyard and ask Luis and his crew if they would like lunch. A sentiment which Eric backed wholeheartedly.

So out of curiosity Sharon made her way towards the trellis and when she arrived she was puzzled by what she had found. All the tools and equipment Luis and his men brought were still there. Yet none of the men could be found. Still in a state of bewilderment she walked deeper among the grapevines. There was no sign of life. Nothing moved, yet the grape plants themselves did look nice and vibrant. The leaves of the plants are large and healthy. The vines are sturdy and strong. There were even budding grapes growing in bunches. Which furthered her confusement and added to her wonder. The grapes looked wonderful, which had to be because something Luis and his group had done, yet where were they and why were they not around to share in this accomplishment. Yet everything turned to complete horror when she felt something coil around her left ankle. She looked down and what she saw made her let out a blood curdling scream for a brief moment. Then something snaked its way around her throat, not only cutting off her ability to breathe but also silencing her in the process.

Eric heard Sharon's scream and was on his feet in a heartbeat. Soon he was rushing out his front door and towards the grapevines. Even though Sharon had stopped screaming abruptly, he was sure that he could find her. He ran quickly to where he knew she had to be and what he saw made him scream out loud himself.

Sharon was now trapped against a trellis, grapevines had pierced her body and were moving like snakes through the holes in her corpse. Blood flowed and dripped onto the ground where it quickly disappeared as if the dirt greedily sucked it down. His wife was dead, which was obvious. Because a large vine grew through one of her eye sockets and out the other. From her mouth hung another vine that had a large bunch of grapes growing at the end.

Eric was frozen in place. A victim of complete fear paralysis. Because of that the vines were upon him in an instant. When he did regain his senses it was too late. The vines had completely wrapped around his arms and were pulling him back towards a trellis. He screamed for a moment yet like his wife before him, a vine wrapped around his neck and squeezed tight. Cutting his scream off in an instant. He could feel the vines press hard against his back as the world around him began to fade to darkness. He struggled for a moment more. Then he was gone.

The vines continued to move and completely destroyed and absorbed the bodies of Sharon and Eric within minutes. Soon there was no sign that they ever were there. The grapevines though, along with the fruit they bore looked incredible. If anyone had come around they would have probably been blessed with a bountiful harvest. That is if the grapes didn't get them first.

THE END

Tobey and The Frog Hopper

Tobey was a fan of the Sandwich Carnival. So much so that he had to attend the annual event as often and as soon as he could when it came to town. He saved up all year and even lied to work on where he was going. Something he was actually surprisingly good at. He had no problem lying to anyone and everyone. Just as long as it got him to the carnival. Of course sometimes his lies left people in compromising situations. Like right now his boss was at work manning the store by himself working a double shift. Missing dinner with his family and kids. Yet, Tobey did not care. He wanted to take in the sights and sounds of the Carnival. Even enjoy the food. Hell it wasn't like anyone was going to die. So hell a nice lie, and here he was at the gates handing over twenty dollars to an elderly woman, waiting for his ticket into the amazing world famous Sandwich Carnival.

The woman looked a little odd and her eyes were bloodshot. Which didn;t really surprise Tobey. Most of the people who worked the carnival had to have at least one or more bad habits.

"Here you go sonny." The woman said as she handed him his ticket.

Tobey excitedly went to thank the woman but paused when he finally got a good look at her face. The skin around the woman's eyes looked incredibly loose and appeared to look as if it was melting. Repulsed by her appearance Tobey quickly turned away and hurried into the Carnival grounds.

He paused for a moment staring up at the darkening sky. The lights from the midway casting a glow, and the enormous Ferris Wheel, lighting up for all to see. It was a beacon of happiness and placed in such a way that no matter where you looked up at you saw the Ferris Wheel. Its lights and music welcoming one and all to the Sandwich Carnival.

Smiling Tobey hurried down the path and made his way towards the ride area just past the midway. He walked by the ferris wheel and saw that people were already climbing into the cars. He could hear chatter above the music from each attraction yet one sound was missing. A sound almost synonymous with the fair. It was the sound of children.

Tobey looked around and saw that there were indeed no children. It puzzled him momentarily, then he remembered that it was a school night and that in this economy people might not be able to take their children to the carnival every night. He was pretty sure that the place would no doubt be packed on Friday. The night where one could enjoy unlimited rides by purchasing a twenty five dollar bracelet. Happy with that excuse he hurried onto the ride area and went to stand in line for the ride he always rode first. The Frog Hopper.

The Frog Hopper was a staple of every Carnival across the land. Even though it went by many names. Sometimes there were larger versions of the drop ride. This one though was just the right height and had a large metal cartoon looking frog at the very top that lit up. Tobey felt it was the perfect starting point for a night of thrills.The ride would take passengers up a good twenty to thirty feet in the air, dropping them repeatedly back to the ground. But before it did that it would only go up halfway before dropping them. It did small little jerks or hops each time it rose up, gradually climbing all the way to the top, then with one final "hop" the ride would go all the way to the top before dropping the passengers all the way back down. Sure it tied your stomach into small knots but Tobey loved it.

There was only one other person in line and he looked over at Tobey and smiled. "Are you ready for this shit?!" The stranger asked.

Tobey smiled, it was always nice to meet a fellow Carnival enthusiast. So he excitedly answered with a "Hell yeah."

The man opened his eyes wide and that was when Tobey noticed the man's eyes were bloodshot. Tobey stared at the man confused then watched as a lone bloody tear fell from the corner of the man's eyes.

"Good I hope so!" The man exclaimed before turning back around.

Tobey wanted to ask if the man was okay, but the carnie controlling the ride called out. "Alright, it looks like you two are the first victims. Take your seats gentlemen."

Forgetting about what he saw Tobey stepped onto the platform and was pleased when the man in line took a seat all the way towards the far right. Leaving the middle seat open. Which was what Tobey was hoping for. Because the middle seat was the seat to have out of the seven on the ride. He sat down and immediately latched the belt across his lap. The carnie then walked over and checked his belt and Tobey did not like the way the carnie smelled. It was like burning meat. Yet the carnie was there and then gone. Taking his smell with him. He didn't bother checking the other guy's belt, instead he walked over to the control panel and turned around, that was when Tobey got a good look at the man's face and he could see that the man's face was red and looked like it was melting as well.

"Alright time to go," The carnie shouted, then he pressed the button bringing the ride to life.

Still uneasy about what he had just seen Tobey braced himself as the Frog Hopper took its first jerking leap upwards.

"Ah yeah you ready for this Tobey!" The guy next to him shouted out.

Tobey turned and gave the guy a confused look. He did not recognize the man at all. He was also pretty sure he did not tell him his name yet somehow the guy knew his.

The ride was moving slowly upward. Which was part of the appeal of the ride in the first place. The slow start made the quick drops all that more thrilling. So Tobey knew there was enough time to figure out how this guy knew his name.

"Uh do I know you?" Tobey asked.

"Nope," The guy answered before adding, "but I know you."

"What," Tobey questioned, "What the hell does that mean?"

"It means I know you are a lying piece of shit," The guy replied.

"Excuse me" Tobey retorted.

"Oh don't act so fucking surprised." The guy continued, "I mean you know you are a liar, you do it so effortlessly. Not caring about the consequences as you do so. You lied to your mom and dad when you were younger, you lied to your girlfriends. Hell, you lied to your boss. Just so you can be here."

Just then the first drop point was met and the ride dropped them towards Earth. Tobey felt his stomach do a little lurch before the first drop was over and the ride started to climb back up. Tobey suddenly felt a wave of anger overtake him as his stomach began to settle.

"What the fuck do you know?" Tobey asked, "You don't know me, you don't know what it's like."

"Are you fucking kidding me right now?" The guy asked with a laugh, "Have you ever told the truth? Do you know the damage your lies cause? Why right now your boss is covering your shift instead of spending time with his wife who just found out she has cancer."

"W-w-what?" Tobey spurted out.

"Yep" The guy answered, "Your boss who put up with a lot of your shit is now stuck at work covering for you. In what is to be the longest night of his life. His wife, waiting at home with no one to comfort her. And sure, sure he will eventually get home. But that's like, heart breaking news you feel me. Imagine what he is going through. Of course with him not being there for her his wife might just decide to end it all."

"Susan wouldn't do that." Tobey responded angrily.

"Oh she wouldn't" the guy replied, "and you know this how. Oh wait, second drop."

As promised the second drop occurred rather quickly and before he knew Tobey was falling back to Earth only falling was not the appropriate word. It felt as if the ride was being pulled towards the ground and at a faster speed than it should. The ride came to a quick and sudden stop and to Tobey it felt as if his entire body was compacted, just for a brief second. He couldn't breathe and everything hurt. He was close to blacking out. He found himself staying conscious and catching his breath just as the ride started to climb back up for its third and final drop. He looked out at the park and what he saw made him start to panic.

Everything was in complete chaos. Practically everything and every ride was on fire. He could see car after car catch fire on the ferris wheel. He watched as a couple of people stumbled out of rides they barely survived. He heard the screeching of metal to his left and turned just in time to see the pirate ship break free of its moorings. Before flying high into the air. There were screams everywhere. He then turned towards the guy on the ride next to him who was now horribly disfigured. He looked more of a monster than man and he was smiling and applauding the chaotic scene that was playing out before them.

"Hell yeah!" The guy shouted before turning towards Tobey, "This is it buddy, all hell is literally breaking loose."

"What the fuck is going on?" Tobey screamed.

"Don't worry you'll find out soon enough," The guy answered, "Now where were we, Oh yeah, your boss's wife, Sharon, she does it you know."

"What?" Tobey shouted out, not really understanding what he was responding to, because right then he was fully in the grip of panic and horror.

"She kills herself," The guy, "Yep and your boss gets to find her body after covering your shift because you fucking lied. You basically caused her death. Your little lie kept her husband from being there with her. But hey you made it to the carnival. You know a carnival that is here for seven fucking days, and hey weren't you off tomorrow?"

Tobey turned his head and looked over and saw that the monster sitting next to him was smiling. Whatever was going on scared the hell out of him, but the monster next to him was right. He was a liar and he never really was one to care about the consequences. Now though they were staring him right in the face. He didn't want to believe the thing sitting next to him. Nothing else made sense honestly. The entire world around him was literally on fire.

"Nothing to say?" The guy asked.

Tobey didn't say anything, instead he looked down as the Frog Hopper rose all the way to the top and stopped. The pause between the last drop was always the longest before the ride plummeted back to Earth. Tobey was so overwhelmed with panic and guilt that he was now surprised to see that the bottom half of the ride was now on fire. He knew any second that he was about to plummet into the flames and he knew without a shadow of a doubt it would kill him. He looked over and that was when he saw that the guy who was on the ride with him was now gone.

Puzzled, Tobey looked around for him and realized that it didn't matter. Everything was gone, or was on fire. Even the ferris wheel,which was still spinning, no longer looked inviting, but was now a flaming wheel of doom. Tobey took one more deep breath and closed his eyes. Waiting for the final drop.

A second later the right fell back to Earth, Tobey felt his body compress, yet he did not scream. He felt the flames begin to torch his body, which didn't matter much because when the ride slammed to a sudden stop practically every organ inside his body burst. Killing him before the flames could devour his corpse.

THE END

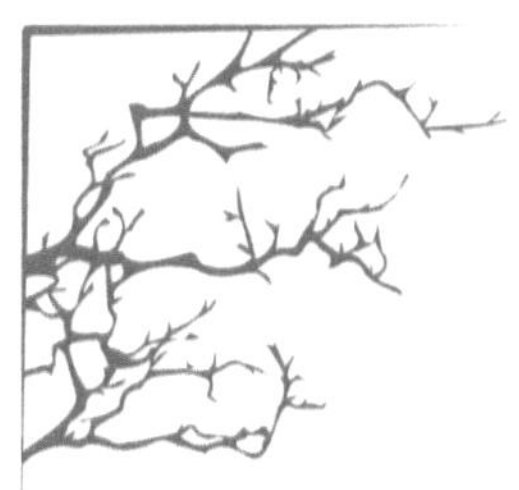

Dynamite

B oom
    Did you hear that
You must have
After all you tore my heart from me

BANG
    Now you heard that
    Sure you did
    You trampled all over me

LEFT ME NOTHING MORE but a mess of explosive emotions

YOU LIT THE FUSE
    Walked away
    Told me I was my own issue
    Not yours, not today
    What am I to do

Explode
And just go everywhere
All at once

POW
  Yep that just happened
  Congratulations
  You left me lying broken and scarred

SO DON'T YOU DARE BE ashamed about the mess you made

02-14-02

....AN OLD ASS ANTI LOVE poem I had lying around, I figured it could live here. A leftover 22 years old. Enjoy!

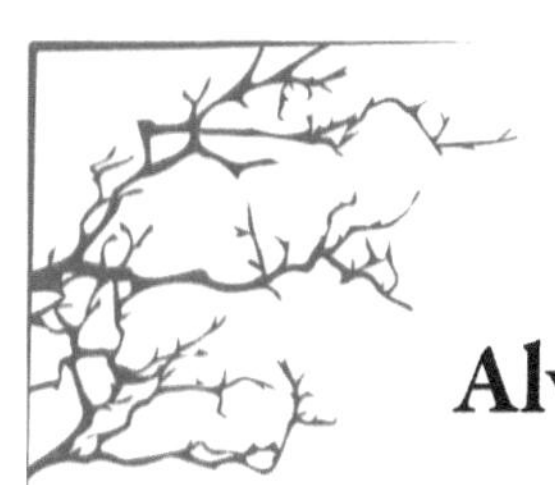

Always and Forever

He watches her. She does not see him. She doesn't know he is there. But he remains vigilant. Making sure no harm would ever come to her. Because he loves her.

He always will.

They were supposed to be married in what feels like a lifetime ago. But alas, that did not come to fruition. Even though what happened was not his fault he still can not overcome the guilt he feels everytime he looks upon her. He promised that he would love her. Always and forever. And he fully tends to fulfill that promise.

Sometimes she senses him. He can tell. Unfortunately she can not see him. No matter how hard she tries. Which hurts him more each time she looks towards him, yet through him just the same.

It is not her fault either. Sometimes life just has other intentions. Sometimes love just isn't enough. Sometimes you have to watch the love of your life move on without.

But he will be there for her. Every step of the way.

He was there when she met the new suitor. A man of means, yet one that was humble. This man held her when she cried, healed her broken heart. And even though he did not want to see her fall in love again he knew that this man would give her everything she wanted and more.

He was there at their wedding. It was a grand affair indeed. The world was theirs and for a moment he felt like he could move on. But he was not ready. He wanted to see if the woman he loved would indeed live the life she deserved to live. The life he wanted to give her yet no longer could.

In life he had tried. In death he would succeed.

Some would say he haunted them. But that was not the case. He merely observed and protected. He did not peep, oh no the private moments of the woman he loved and the man she married was their own. He only observed them when they went about their day to day.

He guarded their home when they were away. Preventing at least three burglaries. He was bound to the world for now. While he could move on. He chose their home as his sanctuary and protected it as such.

And what a nice home it was. Yet such niceties attracted thieves and when these did arrive he showed himself. Terrifying them. The thieves would run from the home lost in terror. Gripped in fear. Being dead has its privileges and scaring the living was indeed a perk. But never them, oh no never them. He was going to make sure she lived her life happy and loved.

Soon the thieves stopped coming, and the house gained a reputation as the criminal underworld talked. A superstitious lot, thieves were. They never tried to break into the home. Leaving it be. He was happy with that, because the woman he loved was now with child.

He wanted to give her a child, but he could not thanks to the accident. Yet this man who loved her was able too. Which made him happy. Yet with this new life being welcomed into the home he was protecting he knew he could not leave just yet.

He did not witness the birth of her child. Again not intruding on private moments. He stayed away. That was after all a moment only for husband and wife. Once the child arrived he took to watching her. Soon he was the daughter's fierce protector.

As she grew so did his love for her. He kept her safe because he knew that the woman he once loved would be devastated if the daughter was harmed. Several times the daughter nearly suffered a horrific accident but he was able to prevent that by catching her with his ghostly hands. A couple of times he was sure that she saw him. But he kept himself from ever revealing himself. Because children reacted differently to something they did not fully understand.

As the child grew the couple grew old as well. Yet he stayed protecting as a lover would. He could not make her happy due to being lost to her so many years ago. Yet his death gave her a life worth living.

Soon the daughter grew. First adolescence. Then teenager. Then adulthood. As an adult the daughter decided to approach the world and go on her own. He watched as the couple, one being the woman he would always love and the man he grew to respect, gave their blessings and out into the world the daughter went.

And he went with her.

The woman he loved had grown and was going to forever have a happy life. Yet the daughter may still need him. So knowing that by keeping the daughter safe the woman he loved would be happy he went.

The daughter was wise and soon began to succeed in a world that had grown big and frightening. Yet he remained on task and before long the daughter herself found love. He then found himself protecting another couple.

He visited the woman he once loved on multiple occasions, yet he was no longer sad. He had fulfilled his promise and with his love kept her safe. He never gave her up. He never let her down.

He loved her. And still did. Maybe she would know what he did for her. Of course he did not mind if she never did. For his love knew no limits. For he watched over a new family. Protected a new home. And a daughter he followed had a son. Which meant an even more grand adventure was on the horizon.

Yes he died ages ago. Never fully understanding life until death. Yet as a ghost he protected all generations of the woman he still loved. And in death he lived a life that anyone so full of love would have been proud to live.

THE END

One Hell of a Rescue

As Ryan sped the ambulance towards Rush Copley Hospital, Brandon sat in the back monitoring the patient who had just opened his eyes.

"Sir!" Brandon shouted, "Sir can you hear me? Can you see me?"

"Holy shit!" Ryan called back, "The guy's awake?"

The patient in question was just discovered outside of a bar in downtown Plano. Passed out on the sidewalk. When they first arrived they found a very weak pulse and assumed the guy had either had a heart attack or too much to drink. Even though everyone outside the bar at the time swore up and down they had no clue who the man was. Regardless they had a duty as paramedics. A heartbeat was a sign of life and they were going to make sure whoever this guy was arrived at the hospital safely. From there it was in the hands of the doctors and nurses. Right now though Brandon was going to make sure this guy stayed alive.

Ignoring Ryan's question Brandon looked down at the man and asked, "Sir can you tell me your name? Where are you from? Hello?"

The man then looked over at Brandon and began to laugh.

The man's laugh was loud and sounding terrifying, it was like a laugh an evil clown would make. Taken back by the sudden laughter Brandon sat back and stared at his patient.

"What the fuck! Is he laughing?" Ryan called back.

Suddenly the man's laughter stopped. He then looked over at Brandon and said, "Well tell him Brandon, am I laughing?"

Once more Brandon's training took over and he ignored the questions being presented to him. Instead he began to ask more questions to the nameless laughing man. "Sir can you tell me your name? Why were you on the sidewalk?"

"Oh my hell" The man chimed in before rolling his eyes, "Does any of that matter, you're still going to try and save his pathetic life. Has it occurred to you that maybe you need to let this one die?"

"Hey Ryan" Brandon called out, "How far out are we?"

"Ten minutes!" Ryan called back.

"Radio ahead and tell them to have someone from Psych standing by," Brandon responded before turning back to the man strapped down on the gurney, "Sir we are going to get you help just keep talking okay."

"For fuck sakes," The man replied, "You know not every life needs to be saved. How many murderers and thieves have you allowed to survive, how many useless lives have you saved?"

Brandon ignored the question and instead checked the straps holding the man in place. The man was obviously out of his mind and he needed to make sure he was secure not just for the safety of the man but for his and Ryan's safety as well.

"Ignoring the question doesn't make it go away Brandon," The man spoke.

Brandon paused, he didn't remember telling the man his name. He took a deep breath and did his best to ignore the man. He obviously had suffered something traumatic and had clearly lost his mind. Trying to get into a battle of wits with a crazy person would not help anyone.

"Oh well," The man said, "Don't answer me if you want. It still will not change things."

What happened next shocked Brandon to his very core.

The man raised up his left arm, at the elbow. His upper arm was strapped down tight so he could only move his forearm and even then he wasn't able to raise it up that far. He then turned to Brandon and said, "Watch this." Then in one quick movement, turned his hand and wrist so violently that both the bones in his forearm snapped.

Brandon watched in horror as the man broke his arm. He immediately noticed that both the radius and ulna bones had snapped and were now poking through the skin at the center of his forearm.

"What the fuck!" Brandon cried out, before letting his training take over. He immediately grabbed the man's wrist and was about to apply pressure, when the man raised his right arm and repeated the process.

"That's better. I bet this guy won't be touching anyone with these hands." The man said. Then he once more began to laugh.

"Ryan see if you can get us there faster," Brandon called out as he began to try to administer some form of help to the man who somehow managed to break both his arms, "Patient just broke both of his arms."

"He what?" Ryan asked.

"Yeah you heard me." Brandon called out,before asking, "Are the cameras back here on?"

"And rolling." Ryan answered.

Brandon replied with a relieved sounding "Good." He then went about the task of trying to not only stop the bleeding but keep the man from further hurting himself.

"Five minutes" Ryan called out, "Do I need to tell them to have surgery standing by."

"Tell them to have everyone." Brandon answered.

The man's laughter had subsided and instead he decided to continue and taunt Brandon.

"You know you are trying to save a pedophile right?" The man asked with a laugh. "Those hands I just broke off at the wrist have damaged and destroyed many a child's innocence and life, yet you try to save him."

Brandon once more ignored the taunting and tried to pack the gaping wounds created by jagged bones. His job was to save lives and the only way he could do that was to keep a level head. He had had many horrible patients in the back of this ambulance and this guy was not going to break him.

"Yeah yeah." The man teased, "The code, you have an obligation to save every life. You don't judge. Blah blah blah."

"That is right sir," Brandon replied.

The man sighed and shook his head before saying. "You are a good man Paramedic Brandon, and it's good men like you that make demons like me exist."

"Sixty seconds" Ryan called out.

"Welp, that's our time together Brandon." The man said, "Look you tried your best but men like this just don't deserve life."

Brandon felt the ambulance come to a complete stop and was quickly on his feet. Ryan was out and running to the back, throwing open the rear doors. Brandon jumped down and together he and Ryan pulled the gurney and the man out of the back of the ambulance. They were joined by a nurse and a doctor who began to acquire what was going on.

"Ooooh let me answer that!" The man called out, "Brandon here and his lead foot buddy, just saved a pedophile. Not judging this man at all. Good men, good men. But I am here to punish this asshole. I mean come on he sticks his dick in children and you're just going to save him. Nope, can't have that." He then let out one more sick bout of laughter before doing something Brandon and Ryan would never forget.

The man quickly began to turn his head to the left. Somehow finding movement even against the restraints. The man was still laughing as he turned his head further and further.

Realizing what was about to happen Brandon rushed forward to intervene, yet he was too slow. There was a loud snap as the man managed to successfully turn his head completely around. Then the laughing just stopped.

"What the hell just happened?" Ryan called out.

His answer was in the form of the nurse behind him fainting.

THE MAN DID TURN OUT to be a pedophile. After interviews with both Brandon and Ryan the police raided the man's apartment. Which happened to be just above Mugshots in downtown Plano. They discovered so much damning evidence in the man's home that people began to praise Brandon and Ryan for not being able to save the man's life.

As for Brandon and Ryan they were cleared of any wrongdoing. The cameras in the ambulance and the statements from the doctor and nurse helped them maintain their innocence,

The incident lived in their head for a brief period but they only talked about it once. It was over dinner and even then they didn't have much to say about. As a matter of fact they ended the whole conversation in a way that made them never want to discuss it again.

"What could possess a man to do that to himself?" Brandon asked.

"Well you heard his laugh," Ryan answered, "It was almost like the devil made him do it. You know."

"Fucking hell." Was all Brandon could say. Both of them feeling chills run down their spine caused by what Ryan had just said.

THE END

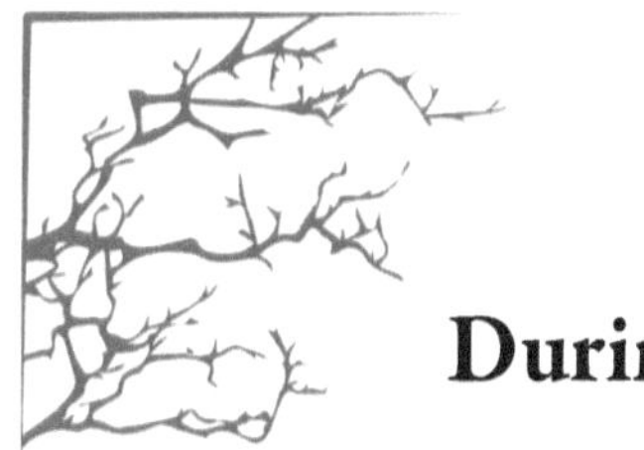

During The Eclipse

The hype behind the solar eclipse on April eighth 2024 was insane, and while Calvin was excited for it he was in no way going to participate in the propaganda behind it. It became an insane marketing ploy to sell t-shirts and ridiculously overpriced cardboard blackout glasses. Of course there were do it yourself options to view the eclipse. Yet Calvin had the best option of all. An old welding mask.

It wasn't that old if he was being honest. It belonged to his dad and was in a box of stuff that he salvaged from his father's house after his father passed away. He planned on selling the items he had collected. But if he was being honest he didn't think that he was ever going to get around to it. Now he was kinda thankful that he hadn't because he did not have to participate in what everyone else was doing. There was no need to purchase anything whatsoever that had to do with the sales blitz surrounding the eclipse.

Of course his feelings on the matter did not stop his wife from purchasing a couple of pairs of the goofy looking glasses. Her excuse being that it was going to be a memorable event and it was something to remember the occasion. To Calvin the memory of watching the damn thing was enough. He did love his wife though so he didn't complain when she brought the glasses home. Just because she did, did not mean he needed to use them.

The week of the eclipse Calvin went hunting for his father's old welder's mask. Finding it almost instantly when he opened the box. Smiling he put it over his face and realized just how dark the world looked when looking through a welder's mask. He adjusted the straps to fit his head and when he was satisfied he took it off and set it on his work bench in the garage. Maybe refusing to wear the glasses his wife purchased seemed childish, yet he could only imagine what his neighbors would think once they saw him walking around with the welding mask.

They would laugh, maybe even find him frightening. Which was fine by him. Calvin didn't mind attracting attention no matter how goofy he looked. Besides, it was all in fun. And he could technically say he did not participate in the dumb marketing device created and controlled by a soulless corporation trying to monetize the eclipse. To him that was silly. Yet it was accomplished and somebody somewhere was able to buy a yacht because of the sales generated by those dumb glasses.

He told his wife what he was doing and she of course found his idea crazy yet harmless as well. All it meant was that his glasses would go unused and probably be worth something in the future. Or if anything a precious memory they could share with their children when they were old and gray. Calvin scoffed at her suggestion but deep down he knew she was right. Who knew what unopened 2024 eclipse glasses would be valued at or even how much sentimental value they may have. Even though in the back of his mind he figured they might be absolutely worthless. To his wife though they would definitely have sentimental value as far as she was concerned.

Also if he was going to be one hundred percent honest. The more he thought about it the more he really wanted to wear that welder's mask to either weird out or amuse his neighbors. He was never going to get another chance to do it so he was really looking forward to it.

THE DAY OF THE ECLIPSE arrived and with it being four hours away the neighborhood was still buzzing with excitement. His neighbors had begun to drag and circle their chairs like wagons around tables where he was sure snacks would be had. He laughed to himself when he wondered just how his neighbors and friends would react when he showed up wearing the welder's mask.

He had made his wife promise to not reveal what he was wearing and she of course asked him to be careful when he wore it. Because she knew just how difficult it was to see out of the mask. Calvin though wasn't too worried he could walk the path to his neighbors house blindfolded if he needed to. Once he got to thinking about it, that's exactly what he was about to do.

His wife had made brownies that she then cut with a circle cookie cutter. Her attempt at a cute snack celebrating the eclipse made Calvin want to roll his eyes. His wife had indeed bought into the whole eclipse hoopla that seemed to be everywhere. But he supported, because he loved her and honestly her brownies were good.

Calvin's wife made her way over to the neighbors thirty minutes before the eclipse was to start and as she left Calvin informed her that he would soon join them and to please not spoil his surprise. She promised she wouldn't and made her way next door.

Calvin snickered as he made his way to the garage and walked over to his father's welder's mask. His hands trembled with excitement and he could not wait to make his neighbors laugh. He had even planned to use exaggerated movements as he approached them. Almost like he was from another planet. Acting as if the eclipse brought him to this world. He was still giggling to himself when he placed the mask over his head and began what should have been a short quick walk to his neighbor's house.

He had promised his wife that he would indeed be careful and he honestly tried to be. Taking each step slowly, yet quick enough to get there before the eclipse actually started. Unfortunately due to the near complete darkness and poor vision he did not see the rake in his yard until it was too late.

The rake was laying in his yard, tines up and when he stepped on the rake head the handle shot up striking the mask between the eyes. The force the rake handle struck the welder's mask was enough to push the mask backwards causing it to press hard on his nose and bring tears to his eyes. He reached up to pull the mask free from his head, unfortunately he was already off balanced so when the rear of his foot made contact with the low wooden barrier his wife had placed to circle her garden that was placed along the side of their house he wound up falling uncontrollably backwards. The back of Calvin's head then made contact with the concrete bird feeder she had placed in her garden. The force behind his fall and the hardness of the bird feeder shattered his skull and sent bone fragments into his brain, killing him almost instantly. He was dead before his body fully settled onto the ground, and he was still wearing the welders mask.

His wife and neighbors did not find him until two minutes after the eclipse had finished, when they realized he had not shown up and decided that maybe they should go looking for him.

THE END

Look Ma, No Hands!

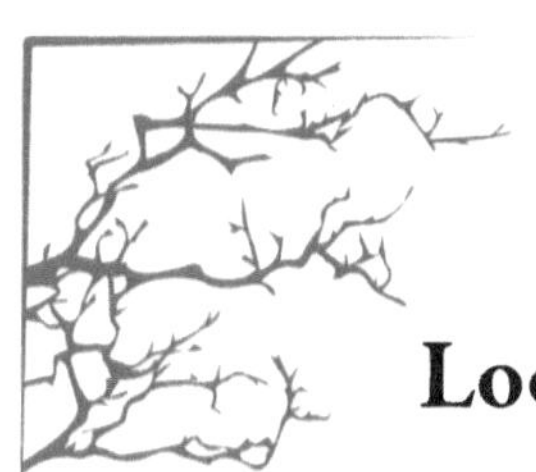

F aster and faster I go
     Where I stop no one knows
Escape the pain
Escape the rain
The demon on my handlebars
Shows me the way

OH WHERE DO I GO
    Oh no I know
    Do I dare tell them
    Should I run from him
    The devil on my shoulder
    Killed my angel today

THE ANGER INSIDE ME
    Burns bright for all to see
    I jump the ramp
    I feel like a champ
    And today the monster I run from
    Leaves me be

Here I go
No one will ever know
I jump the track
I am never coming back
The runaway with no circus
Yet a road to call his own.

03-09-24

....I WROTE THIS POEM WHILE writing "Gary". Sometimes the purest of art hides the darkest of secrets.....

Beware of the Man With the Bowler Hat

Freddie was happily swinging on the swing on the playground in front of Emily G. Johns middle school when he heard the strange whistling come from behind him. He turned and that was when he noticed the strange man wearing a bowler hat walking across the park lot towards the playground.

Freddie had been taught all about stranger danger and he knew that there was something odd about this man. Quickly the young boy jumped off the swing and ran over to the climbing wall and hid behind it. He couldn't shake the feeling that something was about to happen.

Freddie normally came to the playground by himself and today was no different. He sometimes ran into a friend or made friends with the other children on the playground. Today though there weren't any children yet, just a group of six teenagers playing basketball on the basketball court. They of course didn't bother him. Just as long as he stayed off the court and did not interrupt their game. He may be ten but he was smart enough to know not to get in the way of the teenagers and their highly competitive game of three on three. Sometimes he liked listening to them because they always swore and cursed at each other and Freddie was amused by all the new swear words he was learning. Sometimes saying them under his breath and giggling.

The man wearing the weird bowler hat though did not seem to respect the basketball game and walked right onto the court. Interrupting the game and causing one of the teenagers to trip over their own feet and falling on the hard asphalt.

"Hey," One of the teenager's called out, "What the hell are you doing old man?"

"Oh my such poor manners," The man in the bowler hat said, "in my day we respected our elders."

"Man get off the court," another teenager shouted in the direction of the man in the bowler hat.

"You're court?" The bowler hat man asked, "Tsk tsk looks like you children need to learn something the hard way. Fortunately I am in the mood to teach a lesson."

Freddie was peeking out from behind the large climbing rock wall, and he watched as The man in the bowler hat took a quick step towards the closest teenager who happened to be the one who had called the man an old man. He was not moving as if he was old he moved with a scary quickness and then he threw a punch into the chest of the teenager and Freddie watched in horror as the man in the bowler hats fist and arm punched completely through the teenagers chest. Freddie watch blood splatter and that was enough for him to pull back and attempt to make himself as small as possible as he sat down and drew his knees to his chest.

Although he did not see a thing he heard it all. The teenagers began to scream as the man in the bowler hat began to laugh.

"What's the matter?" The bowler hat man called out, "Not so old now am I?"

The taunt was followed by wet tearing sounds, causing Freddie to bring his hands up to his ears and close his eyes. Which seemed worse because even though the wet gross sounds had subsided Freddie could still hear the kids screaming and with his eyes closed his imagination ran wild showing him broken images of what he thought was going on.

After what felt like forever but in reality was just three minutes the screaming had stopped and Freddie slowly dropped his hands from his ears and opened his eyes and what he saw made him urinate on himself.

The man in the bowler hat was now standing directly in front of him and he was covered in blood.

Freddie did what any child would do when confronted with such a disturbing sight. He began to scream.

"Oh my" The man remarked tilting his bowler up slightly, "Sorry chap let me clean myself up a bit."

The man in the bowler hat then snapped his fingers and the blood that was covering him simply vanished.

This did nothing to calm Freddie's fear. Because he just kept screaming and screaming.

"Oh my heavens" The man in the bowler hat remarked. "Silence Freddie, for goodness sake."

Freddie did not know why hearing his name spoken by this murderous stranger caused him to stop screaming but stop screaming he did.

"Good good," The man in the bowler hat continued. "Ok let's make this quick shall we. I am going to allow you to leave and run and have yourself a happy life. All you need to do is one little thing. A favor if you will, can you do that for me Freddie?"

Freddie, still paralyzed by fear, just shook his head up and down.

"Ah wonderful lad." The man in the bowler hat said as he clapped his hands together. "Ok boy I want you to run home and tell everyone you can what you heard and what you will see, and when they ask you who did this you tell them it was me. Can you do that boy?"

Freddie once again shook his head yes.

"I need you to promise me boy," The bowler hat man continued. "I need you to say it, do you promise?"

"I-I-I promise," Freddie stammered with a small hiccup. He was so frightened he was unaware that he was now crying uncontrollably.

"That's a good lad!" The man in the bowler hat cheered, "Welp be seeing you."

Freddie watched as the man then turned around and walked out into the field that was located behind the playground. Then with what looked light a shimmer of heat the man just vanished.

Freddie stood up and stepped out from behind the wall and tried his best to not look at the basketball court yet his eyes moved almost on their own and he found himself staring at the now blood covered court.

It looked as if a massacre had taken place, one that could not have possibly been done by one old unarmed man, but what Freddie saw was indeed horrifying. Body parts were strewn all over the court, there was even a severed arm in a basketball goal. An arm that fell to the ground through the hoop with one loud splat.

The arm was enough for Freddie and he managed to pull his eyes away from the gore soaked basketball court and took off running in the direction of his home. He had a promise to keep, and he was going to keep it. He was going to tell everyone he could about the man in the bowler hat.

Because he did not want what happened to those teenagers to happen to him.

THE END

Getting What They Deserve

B rayden was hiding in the back of his cell trying to make himself as small as possible. He could hear it coming and he knew his days were numbered. They had to be because something had just made its way into the prison that he and his friends had been sent to.

And if he was being honest he knew deep down inside that he deserved whatever was coming his way.

WHAT HAD HAPPENED WAS Frankie's idea. And to be honest Brayden, Cal, and Steven should have known better than to have trusted Frankie. But they were thinking with their dicks and not their brains. Of course it was a believable scenario, hell the stories he heard around campus around girls who grew up sheltered wanting to experience or live out their sexual fantasies would make many a sailor blush. So when Frankie told them that Cindy was wanting to have four guys run a train on her he believed it.

What he didn't know was that Frankie had drugged her and that while Cindy didn't resist she wasn't really aware of what was going on. Brayden knew he should not have participated, but his lust and stupidity overwhelmed so he too took advantage of the near comatose young woman.

After she came to the next morning she immediately felt off and upon discovering that she had been sexually assaulted she immediately contacted authorities.

All four of them did not use protection so there was plenty of DNA evidence against them. The video Frankie took of the event didn't help them as well. Brayden of course guilt ridden over the entire thing took a plea deal. He was still going to wind up in prison but with a lesser sentence and in the protective wing of the prison.

Frankie, Cal, and Steven all received twenty-five years. Brayden got five for his cooperation. And as promised he was shipped to the protective wing that housed other snitches and child molesters were housed. The state of Indiana knew that they could not collect payment from the government if their prisoners kept dying so this was the only logical conclusion was protecting those with the most odds of being murdered by another inmate.

COMFORTABLE AND READY to serve his sentence Brayden began his sentence. One week later news traveled and he was told that Frankie was murdered.

Murdered might have been too gentle of a term because when Frankie's headless corpse was discovered, guards immediately tried to figure out what had happened. When Frankies head was found on the rec room card shelf with his severed penis sticking out of his mouth, Guards really began to wonder.

There was no evidence either. Because the moment before Frankie was presumed killed. The wing he was in suffered a complete and total blackout. The lights and cameras were off for exactly sixty seconds and when they came back on, Frankie was immediately discovered. There were also rumors that Frankies penis and head was not cut off but torn off. Ripped free the other inmates would say.

Figuring that it was a justice killing for Cindy because most inmates do not like rapists, the guards decided to keep a closer eye on Cal and Steven.

Then Steven's corpse was discovered following a complete blackout the following week. His head was torn free as well as his penis. Just like Frankie's. And just like Frankie Steven's head was discovered in an odd place. This time the mop room where the trustees kept their janitorial equipment.

Two weeks in and suddenly two of his friends were slaughtered.

Cal was moved to protective custody while paperwork was pushed through the system to send Cal to the protective wing with Brayden. Brayden didn't really want that to happen but he was prepared to deal with his friend if he needed to.

But Cal never made it out of solitary confinement. His head less and penis less corpse was discovered just three days after Steven was murdered. It also happened after a quick blackout. Cal's head was discovered in a guard tower. This time his penis forced through an eye socket.

BRAYDEN WAS NOW TERRIFIED he refused to come out of his cell and was constantly on watch. They treated Brayden like he was on a suicide watchlist. He was checked on hour after hour. The guards had some crafty serial killer inside the prison walls and they were actually starting to look bad. Not to mention the lawsuits that were probably going to come from the families of the three men that were just slaughtered.

Days passed and Brayden began to feel safe. Then just thirty seconds ago the entire protective wing went dark. So hiding down in the back of his cell hoping to stay out of sight Brayden could hear shouts and see the lights of flashlights as the guards ran towards his cell.

Suddenly the air around Brayden grew cold and he saw out of the corner of his eye and clawed hand from the darkness on the wall. The hand moved further, attached to an arm. Then he saw a hideous almost reptilian-like face grow out of the shadow. He did not see or notice the other hand come behind him until he felt a claw hand grab his crotch. The reptile face turned to him and sneered.

"Cindy says to give you what you deserve." The shadow creature said with a hiss.

Before Brayden could respond he watched as the other hand in front of him suddenly darted out grabbing him by his head. He had just a moment to blink before his head and penis was ripped free from his body.

Brayden's headless corpse was found just like the rest of the rapists. Only his head, complete with penis in his mouth, was discovered on the front lawn of the college campus where they had perpetrated the crime. Stuck on a pike almost as if it was a warning.

THE POLICE INVESTIGATED and for a moment Cindy was questioned and thought to be a suspect. Of course the questioning went nowhere because there was no way a young woman like Cindy could have murdered four men in the way they had murdered while they were in prison.

The police only found one thing that they thought was odd in Cindy's possession but quickly dismissed it. It was a book titled "Shadow Demons and How to Control Them". Dismissing it as pure fantasy. They left it alone, and moved on. Because after all the public really did not care about what happened to four men who raped a young woman.

Hell some even said the boys got what they deserved.

THE END.

The Ballad of Moonbeam
Power Biscuit.

When Maxwell saw his mother come into the front door with the surprise she told him about, he did not know what to do. He just walked over and took the kitten from her and held the little precious animal close.

"Oh mom" He said out loud "I love her"

Maxwell's mother smiled down at her son. She had been watching how well Max had been playing with the neighbor woman's cat and she felt that he would indeed manage a pet of his own just fine.

"Can I show Izzy?" Max asked.

"Of course dear, just be careful around her cat, we don't know how he'll act to a kitten" She answered.

"Oh they'll be fast friends in no time." And then Max was going out his backdoor to show Issadora his new kitten.

He banged on the door and was happy to see Gwendolynn answer it.

"Gwennie" Max called out excitedly.

"Oh hey little Mayhem what do you have there?" She inquired.

Max stepped past Gwendolynn where he held up his kitten to show Issadora who was walking into the kitchen. "It's my kitty"

"Oh my goodness" Issadora exclaimed.

Jynx then walked into the room and immediately took notice of the kitten Maxwell was holding. Jynx hopped up on the counter next to Maxwell and leaned in to sniff the kitten.

The kitten hissed and took a swipe at Jynx who pulled his head back and regarded the kitten with a puzzled look. Then when the kitten calmed down Jynx leaned once more this time the kitten accepted the intrusion. It even playfully batted at Jynx's ears. Jynx then pulled back and sat by the boy still on the counter and meowed at Issadora.

Maxwell turned to Issadora and asked "What did he say Izzy?"

"He asked what her name is," Issadora answered.

Maxwell looked down at the kitten in his arms and then gleefully blurted out "Moonbeam Power Biscuit!" at the top of his lungs.

Gwendolynn and Issadora looked at each other for a minute and then burst out laughing. Max joined them for a bit and then said, "Of course I'll call her Empeebee for short"

This brought another fit of laughter from everyone.

Gwendolynn though suddenly stopped laughing as the room faded away and what she saw was indeed puzzling. She was standing in Maxwell's back yard and there stood the man in the bowler hat. Only instead of sneering or spewing some impending doomsday scenario. He looked scared. She turned and saw that Moonbeam Power Biscuit was now ten times her normal size and she was not hissing but roaring at the man, and then the vision faded. When she snapped back to reality bothe Maxwell and Issadora were looking at her intently.

"What did you see?" Issadora asked.

Gwendolynn walked over and petted the kitten on the head which rubbed its head against her hand then tried to playfully swipe at one of her fingers. "Let's just say this little girl is going to be very important."

Jynx let out a loud meow of approval. Maxwell chimed in "You hear that Empeebee, you're important" He then nuzzled his face on the kitten's face and said "I love you Moonbeam Power Biscuit" This brought a collective awww from the two young women.

Just then Maxwell's mother began to call for him. It was time for supper. "I gotta go bye guys" And he then leaned in to get a big hug from them both, before petting Jynx one last time, then running out the back door to go home.

When he was out of earshot Issadora turned to Gwendolynn and asked "Just how important?"

"Very" Gwendolynn answered before telling Issadora what she saw.

Issadora smiled "Another protector"

"With a silly name," Gwendolynn added.

This brought the girls to a laughing fit so fierce that it brought tears to their eyes.Jynx, though, looked at both of the girls as if they had lost their minds.

THE END

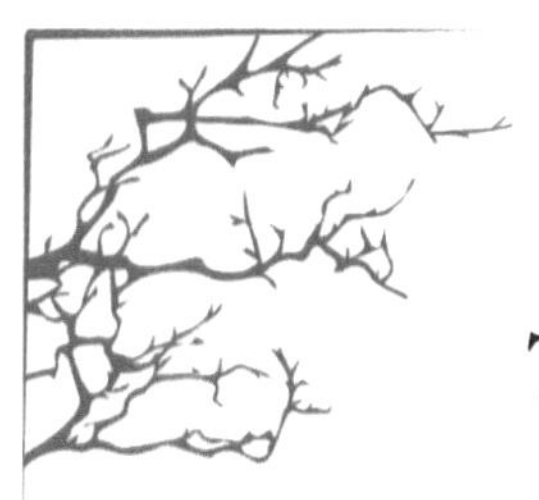

The Cat Knows

The cat watches
	She sees my pain
She purrs in my lap
Until I feel ok again
She is soft
A comfort I can not let go
She knows me
And She will never let me go
I saved her
Now she saves me
I cuddle her when I am sad
She sets my pain free
Pretty pretty kitty
My friend when I have none
She is like my familiar
Like a guiding sun
Hand in paw
Paw over my heart
When my days rough
She shows me where to start
My cat she knows me
And her love is true
My pure blessing
The thing that gets me through
My cat she knows me
And I will be forever thankful

Just have to remember to give her all the scratches
And keep her food bowl full.

07-22-85

...I NEVER MEANT THIS to see the light of day. Yet here it is.In my younger years I wrote so many poems about cats that it is insane. But I will say that I am indeed a cat person. Everyone who knows me knows this. And yeah I have a cat who is my comfort animal. My friend. Dare I say my familiar ... .Welp until next time!!!!!

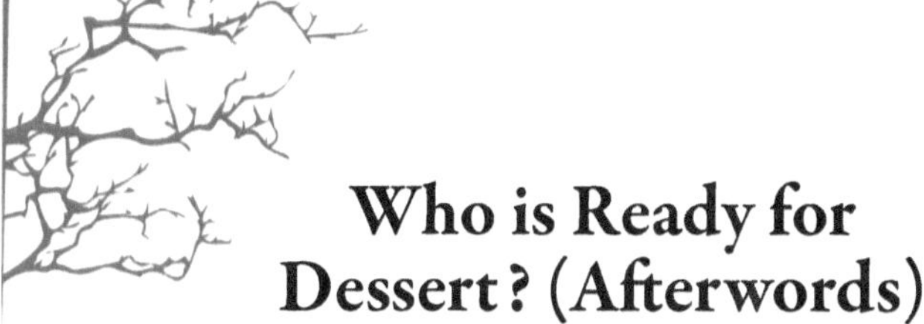

Who is Ready for Dessert? (Afterwords)

Well as promised here are the stories behind the stories. A brief glimpse into what makes my mind click. Or twitch. I dunno you decide and tell me later. But for now let's get this party started.

TOY—-THIS STORY WHICH actually looks like a cross between Freaky Friday and Toy Story was actually inspired by my girlfriend's eldest son. He wrote a unique story for school, about sentient toys fighting a war for a bedroom. It was more complicated than that but it was still a neat little story. There was even a body swapping element at one point. Of course my mind focused on that one section and this story was born. Of course I started it over a year ago and just forgot about it. I never even finished it. I never planned for it to see the light of day and it was going to be left behind. Until now. So here it is. Complete with its own twisted ending. One that I am particularly proud of.

THE OPEN WINDOW—- THIS story was inspired by several different people in my life who always needed to keep their windows open when we went to sleep. It was meant as a joke and grew into this horrific tale of terror. I intended it to be released in my first book but didn't finish it in time. Then I became wrapped up in so many other stories that I just never found the time to complete it. Well now here it is. I hope you enjoyed this story that took me about five years to complete. I know I am glad to have it out of my head.

OF WOLF AND BAT (PART two)—-—One of the oldest stories in the book. I have had this idea since I was fifteen and first started writing. Somehow I just couldn't ever complete it. Then last year I released a poem that took the idea of this story and just made it an artform. Yet the story still lived in my head. Not knowing what else to do I decided to fully flesh out this story. It's just a typical classic monster tale. But I'm happy with it.

THE LAST DAY OF EARTH—- Ah my first apocalyptic story. Originally written when I was sixteen in English class. I tried to tell a story that didn't really tell a story. It was just one man doing his best to cope with the nightmare he is witnessing. The teacher graded it with an A and I thought the story was gone. Until it arrived in an Email with a bunch of my old poetry. Again I didn't know what to do with it, until this year. I touched it up, added some profane language and some modern world elements, added some social commentary and got a nice little gut punch of a tale. Nothing more nothing less.

LITTLE LOST SAINT— This story which expands my Jynxverse, (If you know my work then you know who Jynx is) was originally released as a bonus in my novella what the rain washes away. I will be rewriting that book next year and removing the two short stories at the end. I did not want those stories lost so I decided to put them in this collection. Sure you will get confused if you never read my stories or books about the Jynx the familiar, So hey go out and check out those stories yourself. You will love them I am sure of it!!!

UP FRONT DESIRE—- THIS little story was actually planned for my book "Sick Metal State of MInd" and it was inspired by the song "Last in Line" by Dio. I only include 13 stories in my State of mind series and yet I came up with fifteen stories for that book. So two had to be cut. I chose this one because well I already had two other stories with horrific religious outcomes. A third didn't make sense. Also I myself hated lines, which made this story so easy to write.

CLIFF'S NOTES— AH CLIFF Recker, my police officer character from the long ago completed Lakewood series. This was actually the original ending to the Lakewood series, but it had no impact. It was still a cute tale so I dressed it up and made it an individual story. Sure it's not a horror story but it does tell a good tale. SImple,sweet, and short. Sometimes that's all you need.

THE DEVIL DRIVES A GTO——I loved this story. I loved it when I first wrote it as a Lakewood story four years ago. But after I wrote it, it made no sense. None. Sure it was inspired by a neighbor who drove a GTO through the streets of Lakewood like a mad man. But again made no sense with the direction I was taking the Lakewood series in. So I scrapped it. I revisited it, tweaked it a bit and took Lakewood out of it. And voila. A good tale of bad people suffering bad things.

CATCH——THIS PAST YEAR I released my most personal novel yet, "Gary". It dealt with a lot of trauma I went through as a child. I was so glad to get that novel out of my system. Yet in the process of writing there was one chapter that did not go with the flow. The abuse the character goes through in this book did happen that way. My father was a bastard as I have established in my novel "Gary". This was just another moment of my childhood that he destroyed. Yet I cut this chapter. Still wanting to tell the story of this event I changed and well gave it an ending befitting an abusive father. I changed it from a first person story to this and I am proud of it. Even if it is about an unpleasant memory.

I F@$KING HATE CHRISTMAS—- This mess of a tale was actually supposed to be released alongside a very positive uplifting Christmas story. But my editor said the subject matter was triggering. I listened and shelved the story. Never thinking I would release it. Then I realized I write horror. All my stuff could trigger people. So I decided to just release it alongside all my other long lost stories. Some of you may like it, some may not. But it's off the table and here for everyone. To hate or learn from.

THE WRATH OF GRAPES—- Ever had an idea so stupid you just buried it. Here's mine. An old story that was supposed to go into a recipe book I was creating with my old editor that got cancelled. I found the entire thing dumb so I just didn't do it. But the ending of this story stuck in my head. Haunting my dreams. So I finally just wrote it. It turned out ok. But still a story about murderous sentient grapes is just stupid. Of course I did write a story about killer roses so yeah.

TOBEY AND THE FROG Hopper—- I released my fourth novel this year called "A Carnival to Die For". In it thirteen people barely survive the rides or attractions they are on. (Go read the book to find out what happens to everyone else). There were originally fourteen. My son's mother Deonna suggested I write a story about the Frog Hopper ride. For some reason I just felt thirteen people were easier to manage than fourteen. But I still had this chapter almost done. So I gave it a final ending. Made it its own little story of one guy's experience at the Carnival that I wrote about. It works. I liked it and now it will not be lost.

Always and Forever— This sad little love story based on the song "Never gonna give you up" By Rick Ashley, was cut from my book Strange 80's state of mind. I didn't like how sappy it was and it just didn't really feel like it meshed with what I was doing. I never even attempted to finish it. Until I found it. Almost begging me to finish it. So I did. It might not be the best story but it definitely pulls at the heartstrings. It deserves to be read and well now it has been.

ONE HELL OF A RESCUE—- This little creepshow story actually was going to be a chapter in an upcoming 4/26 novel that I cancelled. It was to play a bigger part and served as the opening of that novel. Yet I just did not like the direction I was going with the characters so I just made it its own story about my two paramedic characters. I mean they deserve something to do that's not 4/26 related right?

DURING THE ECLIPSE—- This silly story that is really a black comedy misadventure more than anything is really the newest story in this book. I conceived it the day of the eclipse that took place on April 8th 2024. While I myself was running around wearing a welder's mask. It was honestly just a silly little story with an abrupt ending I have come to enjoy writing. I figured including it here would make sense. Seeing as how it was written and didn't quite have a home yet. Plus its short nature just seems like it would be perfect padding for any anthology. It stays around just enough to make the reader go, "What the Hell?"

BEWARE OF THE MAN WITH the Bowler Hat—- This story cut from the pages of my Lakewood series was actually inspired by readers of the first book saying my villain was too generic. They even complained about it online. So I had him terrorize and murder children. Feeling I went too far and that my dark joke wouldn't be understood, I quickly removed the story. Even though we all love a good dark boogeyman story.

Getting What They Deserve—- Ah yes the second story pulled from My "Sick Metal State of Mind" book. Based off of the song "You Got Another Thing Coming" by Judas Priest. This story was simple and to the point. Call it the demonic version of "Fuck Around and Find Out" I mean a monster intentionally imprisoning itself to get it's hands on a group of rapists. I mean that's justice. And horror. Who said monsters can't do no good?

THE BALLAD OF MOONBEAM Power Biscuit—- This story was another bonus story released at the end of my novella "What the Rain Washes Away" and it was meant as a joke. As I mentioned earlier this little out of place story that only people familiar with my work would understand, along with another story are going to be removed from that novella when I rewrite it next year. Still not wanting to lose that story I am including it here for all of you to enjoy. Or question my intelligence. Honestly this story is so goofy I could just let it go away but my son who was 11 at the time helped me write it. So long live Moonbeam Power Biscuit!!!

NOW SOME OF YOU MAY wonder why the poems themselves didn't have a story behind them. Well that's because I gave a brief snippet behind each poem after the date I wrote them. I have poetry everywhere and every now and I have enough to release a book. I had these six lying around and thought why not, a little special gift for my readers. Eighteen stories and six poems. Wow, generous right. I'm kidding, but hey hopefully you enjoyed this little anthology of mine.

WELL THERE YA GO. I do hope you enjoyed our time together and I hoped I answered all your questions. I hope you licked your plates clean. Anyway....Until next time, love you guys!!!!!

About the Author

Kevin began writing short stories when he was an awkward teenager living in a small town in Alabama. Now as an awkward adult, Kevin now lives in a small town in Illinois and still writes short stories. Only this time he is releasing his madness into the world.

Read more at https://books2read.com/rl/WYaLOW.